David & Goliath

by

Diana Stout

Cover design Cover Bistro

ISBN-13: 978-1717397454 (Paperback)
ISBN-10: 171739745X

Introduction

I grew up fascinated with the written word. I'd read by pen flashlight and when those were taken away, I'd read by the street light that streamed through the window. I'd read while walking home from school, between classes, in the car, and any other spare moment. I checked out library books a dozen at a time.

And then I fell in love with movies. I loved going to our small-town theater and especially enjoyed watching the old black and white movies on television. *The Uninvited* with Ray Milland was my favorite for the longest time. I became a movie junkie, loving the classic and movie stars of the past. Even today, movies starring Gregory Peck, Susan Hayward, Rock Hudson, Doris Day, Charlton Heston, Cary Grant, Clark Gable, and Maureen O'Hara are still my favorites.

A perfect writing marriage for me occurred when I learned how to write screenplays. This medium was pure joy. I could better write the visual I saw in my head.

My hope is that you'll enjoy reading one of my scripts as much as you do my novels, novellas, short stories, or plays.

My dream is that somewhere along this fabulous writing journey that one of these published scripts will end up in the hands of someone who sees a movie worth producing--a life-long dream for this writer.

Enjoy!

Diana Stout
May 9, 2018

DAVID & GOLIATH

EXT. NEW ORLEANS - NIGHT - FIFTEEN YEARS AGO.

City is quiet. Few cars on street. A POLICE SIREN WAILS.

INT. UPSTAIRS ROOM

No windows. Walls and floor painted black. Weird white voodoo markings painted on floor.

Only light, a bare bulb overhead.

Old wrought iron-frame bed sits in a corner.

On wall above headboard, hangs wooden cross with DAMBALLAH (a snake, the god of gods in voodoo religion) twisted around the cross.

On the bed, a thin mattress covered with plastic, hands and feet tied is JESSICA, 10, blonde. Disheveled, gagged, eyes huge. Wears a pair of red shorts, red and white striped short-sleeve top.

In b.g. soft SOUNDS OF DRUMS, VOICES CHANTING, PRAISES TO DAMBALLAH.

A MAN, dressed in black, head in shadows, back to us, steps into view. Jessica struggles. The man's body fills the screen.

                                                    CUT TO:

EXT. DEEP BAYOU WOODS - NIGHT

Wispy clouds, a sliver of moon. Pine and cypress trees with hanging moss cast giant shadows.

Rarely used dirt road, more grass than road, two slashes of dirt ruts.

Frog CROAKS. Alligator bellows out a MATING CALL.

Headlights cut into the night.

A car STOPS on the road.

The man, face and head in shadows, gets out, snaps on surgical gloves, goes to the trunk, opens it.

Hauls girl out of trunk. Stands her up. Hands and feet tied, she stands quietly, head hanging, cries silently though still gagged. Hair a mess, bruise on her jaw, clothes rumpled.

He unties her, removes gag. She doesn't move, doesn't make a sound though tears stream down her face. She trembles at his touch.

He slides a bracelet, two silver snakes intertwined, onto her arm. He points to the forest, indicating she's to go.

When she doesn't move, he turns her around, pushes her forward gently.

Over her shoulder, she glares at him, then runs.

He reaches into the trunk. Pulls out a leather rifle case.

He glances at her, unzips case, pulls out a powerful rifle with night scope. He raises the rifle to his shoulder.

The girl in his night-scope, he follows her for a few seconds, then FIRES ONE SHOT. Into the back of her head.

BODY CRASHES into the BRUSH.

SILENCE.

One by one, frogs CROAK again, LOUDER this time.

He lowers the rifle, places it back in case, zips it shut, closes trunk, picks up a fresh pine limb, loaded with needles.

SCRAPES the road, erasing all foot prints, gets into car, sweeps away last footprint, tosses the branch away.

Removes gloves, tosses on seat next to a police badge, shuts the door and DRIVES OFF.

CUT TO:

EXT. DEEP BAYOU WOODS - DAY

Several patrol cars parked alongside road. Policemen, in shirt sleeves, perspiring heavily, mill around.

Noses wrinkle from the stench. Two rookies wipe their faces against their sleeves. FRISCO, big, mean looking, speaks without emotion. And, JACK MAISNER, a cocky lady's man.

                    JACK
          Christ, if it's this hot in January, what's
          summer gonna be like?

                    FRISCO
          Hell.

They turn as two unmarked patrol cars pull up.

Two young plain-clothes cops emerge from one car, JASON DAVID and LARRY,
both mid-to-late 20s.

CARLIN GUIDRY (40 something, not too out of shape, attentive but at ease) and
Jason's father, MAURY DAVID (40 something, his gaze taking in everything)
emerge from the second car. Partners since rookies, now detectives.

All four walk to the crime scene, passing the first two cops.

                    GUIDRY
          Jesus. What a smell.

                    MAURY
               (to Jack & Frisco)
          She been identified yet?

                    JACK
          No.

                    LARRY
          Photos taken?

                    FRISCO
          Yes.

                    GUIDRY
          Coroner here?

                    FRISCO
          On his way.

Guidry, Maury, Jason and Larry are at the body.

Jason and Larry react to the smell. Faces scrunch up. Larry covers his mouth. Jason
holds his breath. Guidry bends over the girl and turns her over. Larry turns away.
Jason gasps, takes a few steps away, forced to stop, bends over, and PUKES.

Maury, hearing him, turns, walks over to him. Jason rises, wiping his mouth.

                              MAURY
                    You'll get used to it, son.

                              JASON
                    She's just a kid, Dad, no older than Silky.

In the background, near the road, an officer kneels to the ground. He looks up and
shouts in Maury's direction.

                              OFFICER
                    I found something!

Maury, Guidry, Jason, and Larry scramble to where the officer is. On the ground is a
shell.

The photographer done, Guidry takes a pen from his pocket, slides it in the shell and
picks it up. Maury holds out a plastic bag. Guidry drops it in. He looks to Jason, then
to Maury.

Maury nods. Guidry hands the bag to Jason.

                              GUIDRY
                    Wanna crack at solving it?   You and Larry?

                              JASON
                    You mean--?

                              MAURY
                    Congratulations, boys. The Captain officially
                    made you our newest detectives. We'll be
                    working as a team.

INT. POLICE REPORTING ROOM - SEVERAL DAYS LATER

Second story of the 8th District New Orleans Police Department.

Desks butted together. Cops sit in front of computers. One on a manual typewriter.

In one corner, a huge coffee urn, garbage overrun with Styrofoam cups litters the
floor.

Jason, at a desk, goes through a file. The shell and bracelet are on his desk. Guidry
and Maury enter, head for the coffee pot.

                              MAURY
                    Any leads, son?

                    JASON
          Not yet, Dad. Her name is Jessica Horton. A
          local. Reported missing two days before she
          was killed.

                    MAURY
          You'll find the killer.

                    JASON
          Got to. I have your reputation breathing
          down my neck.

He grins at his dad, picks up the shell, fingers it, studies it. Maury picks up the
bracelet, looks at it.

                    JASON (CONT'D)
          We've got some great leads, though. There's a
          new houngan emerging.

Maury hands the bracelet to Guidry.

                    GUIDRY
          Voodoo?

Larry joins them.

                    LARRY
          An evil one so the gossip goes. After we
          verify these leads, we'll know who it is.

Maury and Guidry look at each other.

                    MAURY
               (winks at Guidry)
          Cocky, ain't he?

Guidry laughs.

                                                            CUT TO:

EXT. NEW ORLEANS - DARK ALLEY - NIGHT

Deep shadows, TWO MEN talk.

                    FIRST MAN
          He'll be there. The rest is up to you.

An envelope thick with money passes between them.

                         SECOND MAN
              Tonight.

                                             CUT TO:

EXT. CONVENIENCE STORE - LATER THAT NIGHT

Bright interior lights beacon out into the black night.

INT. CONVENIENCE STORE

Empty except for CLERK, too young, too inexperienced to be left alone this late.
He makes faces into one of the security cameras, watches himself on screen.

Bell above the door JANGLES. Clerk is slow to turn. When he does, he faces the
barrel end of a gun.

ROBBER'S hands and face concealed by gloves and mask. Brown eyes and white
skin around eyes.

                         ROBBER
              Don't look at me!

Clerk immediately looks down, shaken.

                         ROBBER (CONT'D)
              Open the register.

Tosses a bag onto the counter.

                         CLERK
              Yes, sir.

Clerk obeys, opens it.

Drawer slides open. Both hands pull out money.

EXT. STORE

Two unmarked police cars pull up to the building's side. No lights, no sirens, out of
view of clerk and robber.

Jason and Larry from one car, Guidry and Maury from the second. Normal talk.

Not aware of inside event.

Guidry is first around the corner, followed by Larry close behind him. Guidry sees the robber without him seeing Guidry. He retreats, drawing gun and pushes Larry back.

                    GUIDRY
          Robbery.

                    (TO MAURY)
          Call it in.

                    (TO JASON & LARRY) (CONT'D)
          Circle round to the other side.

The two disappear around the building. Seconds later, Guidry see them, and signals for them to wait. Maury joins Guidry.

Entrance door bursts open. Robber runs out.

                    GUIDRY
          Stop!   Police!

Robber fires wildly, from side to side. Won't be taken.

All four return fire.

                                        CUT TO:

EXT. CEMETERY - DAY

Sea of police uniforms circle a casket, minister, and members of family.

Up close, Larry, arm in a cast.

MRS. DAVID stands behind her husband's wheelchair, her hand on his shoulder. Next to her is 10-year-old SILKY DAVID, Jason's sister. She stares at the casket, refuses to cry. Angry.

Maury's leg propped up and in a cast. He pats wife's hand. Grim expressions, but no tears.

Guidry stands next to them, his arm around his son, NEIL, 12, slim, tall for his age.

Seated, in a chair next to Maury, in front of Silky is JENNY, extremely pregnant. She gets up, lays a white rose on the casket.

GUN SALUTE FIRES. Smoke from the guns surrounds Silky and the other mourners. A folded flag is given to Jenny as she stands at the casket.

As one, the crowd turns, and disperses.

Jenny turns, pauses, her head down, a hand to her face. She starts to sob. Mrs. David goes to her, put her arm around her and leads her away.

                              GUIDRY
          Maury, I--

                              MAURY
          It wasn't your fault, Guidry. Stop blaming
          yourself.

                              GUIDRY
          The boy was a rookie.

                              MAURY
          No different than when we started. If you
          hadn't taken that--

His chin trembles, and the next word is grated out.

                              MAURY (CONT'D)
          --monster out, we all could have been... He
          killed my boy. One bullet. At least he didn't
          suffer. If that bastard weren't already dead,
          I'd--

Guidry puts a hand on Maury's shoulder and squeezes.

Guidry grabs the wheelchair handles, turns the chair and the two men and Neil leave. Silky remains. Standing, staring at the casket.

Neil stops, turns, and starts to go back. Guidry sees him.

                              GUIDRY
          Come on, Son. Leave her alone. She needs a
          minute.

Silky stares, then finally steps forward. Puts a small hand on the shiny wood. One lone tear trails down her face.

                              YOUNG SILKY
          Bye, Jason.

She steps back, wipes the tear from her face, takes a deep breath, turns, walks away.

In the distance, Guidry stands at the limousine where her father and mother and Neil are seated inside, waiting for her.

CUT TO:

Cars pull away. Soft wind blows. Moss on live oaks swing in the breeze. Suddenly, it stops. Totally. Everything comes to a standstill. Not even a bird twitters.

The cemetery is PANNED. Last car exits the area.

CLOSE ANGLE - COFFIN

Among the flowers on the coffin is something that wasn't there before. Sprigs of weeds and the skull of a small mammal.

INT. DAVID'S HOME

Officers, friends mill around, plates and drinks in hand. Mood is somber, quiet talk.

Silky looks even smaller among the adults. She hears snatches of conversation as she walks through the crowd:

>   OLD WOMAN
>   Such a good boy, mowed my yard every week.
>   Wouldn't take any money.

>   MAN
>   Never saw him talk back to his mother or
>   father. Ever. Not like other kids today.

>   OFFICER
>   A shame. His knee blown out, the old man is
>   done. The boy was the last of the line. Hard
>   to believe there won't be any more David's--

>   YOUNG SILKY
>   That's not true!

All heads turn toward her.

>   YOUNG SILKY (CONT'D)
>   I'm a David.

She looks up at these men in uniform, determination strong on her face.

>   YOUNG SILKY (CONT'D)
>   One day I'll be just like you. A cop.

The crowd parts and suddenly there's her father, in his chair. Guidry stands behind him. Her mother at Maury's side, her face ashen.

13

                    OFFICER
                 (to Maury)
            Tis just a response.

                 ANOTHER OFFICER
            Only natural, it'll pass.

                 YOUNG SILKY
            And I'll be better than all of you!   You wait
            and see!

                    MOTHER
            Don't let her Maury. She can't. It's bad
            enough the men in the family have to die.
            Must the women die too?

Her mouth tight, she puts her hands to her face, starting to weep. Guidry takes her in his arms, turning her from Silky, leading her away.

Maury stares at his daughter. Silky returns the stare, not blinking, unwilling to back down.

                    MAURY
            Don't do this to your mother.

                 YOUNG SILKY
            You did it to her first.

She turns, pushing her way past through the forest of uniforms. Finally, she's through and makes her way into the--

INT. KITCHEN

--where the women are busy with the food. No one sees her. She moves through the room, going out--

EXT. OUTSIDE

--through the back door.

She stands on the porch. Arms wrapped around herself, she stomps her foot. Mad, angry emotions on her face.

Neil steps onto the porch. He's followed her. He's concerned.

                 YOUNG NEIL
            Silky?

Silky wilts a little, shoulders slumping, eyes close, then open, readying herself for a new attack, disgusted that she's been followed. She spins on her heel to face him.

                    YOUNG SILKY
          What do you want, Neil?

Neil takes a step back, holding up a hand as if to ward off an attack.

                    YOUNG NEIL
          Whoa. I'm your friend remember?

                    YOUNG SILKY
          Then leave me alone.

                    YOUNG NEIL
          You'll make a great cop.

Silky stares at him, tilts her head, almost as if she doesn't hear him. The corners of her mouth lift a little.

                    YOUNG SILKY
          The best ever. We both will. They'll see.

                    YOUNG NEIL
          Wanna go for a walk?

She nods.

Together they descend the steps and walk toward the trees at the back of the property, walking side by side, not touching. Finally, Neil puts an arm around her shoulder.

Beat.

Silky leans into him, resting her head on his shoulder, her arm going around his waist as they walk on.

Guidry steps onto the porch, spots the children, starts to call out, then stops, just watches them.

                                        FADE OUT:

                                        FADE IN:

EXT. NEW ORLEANS - EARLY DAYBREAK - PRESENT DAY - 15 YEARS LATER

INT. SILKY'S APARTMENT - HALLWAY

A key is INSERTED into the entrance door lock, the knob turns, and a grown-up SILKY (25), a beauty with blond hair, wearing uniform, enters the room.

She throws keys and badge on entry table by door. Thumbs through mail in her hand.

Freezes. A folded note. She unfolds. Reads it.

Tosses it into a basket filled with other typed notes like it. She turns and locks several locks on door.

CLOSE-UP ON TYPED NOTE: I'm still watching you. Why didn't you invite me to share your salad last night?

She moves into the--

INT. SILKY'S LIVING ROOM

Goes to window, cranks up the window air conditioner. Looks out through the top window pane, over the top of the air conditioner, gaze skimming windows in building across the road.

INT. STRANGER'S APARTMENT

POV through a camera lens of Silky, looking down into her apartment. Snaps pictures in quick succession.

INT. SILKY'S LIVING ROOM

She sticks out her tongue.

She unbuttons her shirt, pulls it out from pants, revealing a T-shirt underneath. Pulls it out of pants, turns, lifts the back. Enjoys cold air on bare skin.

Moves across room. Wall displaying her history is PANNED:

--Police graduation, holds diploma, parents on either side.

--Newspaper articles with her picture show her rise in the force.

--Jason, her father and Guidry, at the shooting range, all grinning, all holding up their targets and the targets all shot cleanly through the heart and head.

--Article with a headline of valor for rescuing a family from a burning car.

INT. BEDROOM

Morning light streams through window. Staying away from window, removes holster and hangs on closet door.

Returns to--

INT. SILKY'S LIVING ROOM

--moves through room, into--

INT. SILKY'S KITCHEN

--opens refrigerator, grabs filtered water container, pours a tall glass. Gulps half of it down.

INT. STRANGER'S APARTMENT

Camera clicks rapid succession following movement.

Silky goes to L.R. window, looks straight at camera, closes blinds.

Then, bedroom blinds close.

INT. SILKY'S BEDROOM

Pitch-black. CLICK. Bedside lamp provides light.

INT. SILKY'S BATHROOM

Steam filled. Silky in shower. Rinsing off, she leans against the wall, tired. Finally, she turns off the water.

INT. SILKY BEDROOM

In s sleep shirt, legs bare, Silky throws off the blanket, using only a sheet, turns off light.

EXT. GARDEN DISTRICT

Quiet street. Twittering birds welcome the day. Old two-story homes with big porches and iron-wrought fences line the street.

A sprinkler comes on in one yard.

Plump, sixty-plus woman opens front door of her house, wearing sleeveless nightgown, open lightweight robe, and fluffy feathery flip-flop slippers. Reaches for paper on porch.

A cat scampers out the door, runs between the woman's legs.

Startled, she straightens forgets paper, lets go of screen door, THUMPS closed, chases after the cat.

                    WOMAN
          Scarlett!   Come back here you bad pussy.
          Come back here!

Her voices goes up several octaves.

                    WOMAN (CONT'D)
          Here kitty, kitty, kitty.

The cat disappears into bushes lining the iron-wrought fence.

The woman peers through them, moving branches, not willing to get scratched.

                    WOMAN (CONT'D)
          Come Scarlett. Time for breakfast. Your
          favorite. Sardines.

The cat meows further down the row. The woman smiles, straightens, zeros in on the sound.

Shuffles down a few yards. Bends over, rear in the air, parts the bushes, calling--

                    WOMAN (CONT'D)
          Here kitty, kitty--

WOMAN'S POV - UNDER THE BUSHES

--a hand, to an arm, to a young woman (mid 20s), slim, blond, eyes open but unseeing lies face up on the ground.

She's nude except for a silver bell on a silver chain around her neck.

                                        BACK TO SCENE

Startled, frightened, the woman stumbles back, falls on her butt, tries to scream, but can't. Claws to a standing position.

Screams at the top of her lungs. Runs toward house.

EXT. NEW ORLEANS INTERNATIONAL AIRPORT - LATE
AFTERNOON/DUSK

Airplane lands.

INT. POLICE PRECINCT - LOCKER ROOM

Officers arrive, some leave.

RANDY COOPER (same coloring as Silky, better than average looks, late 20s)
catches up to Silky, throws his arm around her shoulder casually. Silky dressed like a
hooker, hair teased, piled haphazardly but sexually on top of her head. Short skirt,
skimpy top, shows off her ample chest.

                         RANDY
              Nice outfit.

                         SILKY
              No.

                         RANDY
              You haven't even heard--

                         SILKY
              That you want me to work your shift
              tomorrow night.

                         RANDY
                   (grinning)
              Yeah, that's right.

Silky reaches up, picks up his hand by a few fingers and throws hand aside.

                         SILKY
              You lose.

Randy halts, a stunned almost hurt expression on his face.

                         RANDY
              Aw, Silky, don't do this to me.

                         SILKY
              After what you did to me?

                         RANDY
              Aw, come on. You're not going to hold that
              rabbit thing against me forever, are you?

Silky stops, turns around, facing Randy head-on, forcing him to stop in front of her.

Though she's a full foot shorter, she starts poking him in the chest with a finger, a bright red painted nail forces him to step backward.

She keeps poking, moving forward, following him. Her jabs getting harder and harder.

                    SILKY
          Rabbits, slime-ball. Rabbits. Lots of them. In
          my apartment. They chewed everything. Not
          to mention all those little pellet presents they
          left everywhere. You even put one in my
          microwave and one in my underwear drawer.
          You're despicable.

She spins on her heel, leaving him open-mouthed and apologetic.

                    RANDY
          Aw, Silky, it was two months ago! What if I
          promise no more pranks?

                    SILKY
               (over her shoulder)
          Too late.

At their perspective lockers, Silky quickly spins open the combination lock. Randy just stands there watching... waiting... hoping.

                    RANDY
          What if I--

                    SILKY
          Never.

She snaps the locker open, tosses her purse inside, snaps it shut, spins the lock.

                    SILKY (CONT'D)
          Sweetie.

She walks around corner and is gone. Randy opens his locker. Jaw drops.

Locker filled with whipped cream.

                    RANDY
          Fuck me.

                    O.S. MALE VOICE
          Can't. Already got a date tonight.

Jack Maisner, now early 40s, comes around corner, approaches, looks at locker.

                    JACK
          Ain't that sweet.

Jack sticks his finger in it, pulls out a dollop of white, sticks it in his mouth, disappears where he came from.

Other COPS come and go. Hardly anyone notices. Business as usual.

                    RANDY
          (yelling loud enough so Silky
           will hear him)
          This is war, COUSIN!

Randy slams locker shut.

Whipped cream splashes everyone and everything nearby. Others GROAN, MOAN, GRUMBLE, VOCALIZING disapproval.

Randy stalks off, passes Larry (now mid-30s) opening his locker. Water balloons fall out, splashing at his feet.

Beat.

He looks down at soggy pant legs, shoes and socks, water everywhere.

                    LARRY
          Mahoney, you're a dead man!

INT. NEW ORLEANS INTERNATIONAL AIRPORT - NIGHT

DONOVAN (GOLIATH) O'ROARKE, 30-something, tall, wide-shouldered man, better than average build, comes down the ramp, easily shoulders his only luggage, a large duffel bag.

Passes through throng of passengers, some meeting waiting people: welcomes, hugs, kisses.

Passes through them as if he doesn't see them. Gaze straight ahead, steps steady, unfaltering.

INT. NEW ORLEANS INTERNATIONAL AIRPORT

Donovan stops at newspaper stand, picks up a paper and pulls out a dollar, lays on counter, starts to walk away.

                    YOUNG CLERK
          Don't you want your change, mister?

                    DONOVAN
          Keep it. Start a college trust fund.

INT. POLICE PRECINCT - CONFERENCE ROOM

The room is blackboards, tables and chairs.

Rollcall. Silky and Randy stand side by side, each leaning against the wall.

The SERGEANT gives a rundown of the day's events for the night crew.

EXT. NEW ORLEANS INTERNATIONAL AIRPORT

Donovan hails a taxi. One pulls up. Donovan tosses his bag into the back seat, following it. Taxi pulls out and into traffic.

INT. POLICE PRECINCT - CONFERENCE ROOM

Rollcall and instructions over. Chairs SCRAPE the floor as cops rise.

Those leaning against the wall, straighten. Silky adjusts her bra, revealing more cleavage, getting ready for her role.

Jack walks past her.

                    JACK
          Need any help?

                    SILKY
          Not in your lifetime.

He's gone. Randy takes his place. She mumbles to herself.

                    SILKY (CONT'D)
               (continuing)
          Pervert.

                    RANDY
          I try. Go ahead with the others. I'll be right
          there.

He holds up some papers in his hand.

                    RANDY (CONT'D)
              (continuing)
          Guidry wants this right away.

In full character, Silky cracks her gum.

                    SILKY
          Partner, just don't keep me waiting too long.
          Otherwise I may have to find me another
          Sweetheart.

She pats his cheek and leaves, not noticing that every other male stops to admire the
saucy way her tail moves provocatively in her short skirt and heels. Randy shakes his
head.

                    LARRY
              (to Randy)
          Shame you two are related. You'd make a cute
          couple.

EXT. POLICE PRECINCT - NIGHT

Located in the heart of the French Quarter, precinct is a tall stucco building,
surrounded by buildings with iron wrought porches.

Lots of tourists, couples with arms around each other, some drink from plastic cups,
others carry numerous shopping bags.

Party atmosphere. Pre-Mardi Gras.

No one pays attention as a cab pulls up to the curb.

Donovan exits, shoulders duffel bag, pulls a few bills out his pocket, pays the driver.
Cab moves off.

Donovan looks up at the building, then at the neighborhood.

INT. POLICE PRECINCT

Donovan stops at the public information desk and is directed toward the staircase.

INT. POLICE PRECINCT - REPORTING ROOM

Donovan stops at first desk in the room full of desks. A cop points toward the back
of the room at the closed in windowed office of Carl Guidry, Captain.

Donovan heads that way, passing Randy at a desk, who slaps the side of a printer.

Donovan knocks on Guidry's partially open door.

Guidry signing papers. He's aged over the years--hair thinner, bit of a paunch.

> GUIDRY
> (without looking up)
> Yeah?

> DONOVAN
> Captain Guidry?

Guidry's head lifts up, puzzled.

> DONOVAN (CONT'D)
> Donovan O'Rourke.

Guidry jumps up out of his chair, goes around the desk, hand out.

> GUIDRY
> Glad to see you. How was your trip?
> Uneventful, I hope?

> DONOVAN
> I've had smoother.

> GUIDRY
> Air around here can be turbulent. You'll learn
> to like it.

Randy knocks on the door and enters.

> RANDY
> Sorry to interrupt. He hands Guidry a file.

> GUIDRY
> Randy, this is Donovan O'Roarke. From New
> York. Randy Cooper. The two men shake
> hands.

> RANDY
> (to Donovan)
> Hope you like things hot. Weather can be a
> killer here.
> (to Guidry)
> Gotta go meet the team.
> (to Donovan)
> See you later, Donovan.

Randy leaves. Guidry guides Donovan out the door.

GUIDRY
Let me give you a quick tour of the place, get
you your badge, and then you can start work
tomorrow. Take it easy tonight.

                                        DISSOLVE TO:

EXT. POLICE PRECINCT - NIGHT

Donovan leaves the building, shoulders his bag, walks down the street, passing a
dark alley. HEARS A GROWL. He freezes.

DONOVAN'S POV - LOOKING DOWN ALLEY

A dog, terrier, stands in the shadows. Feet spread, snarls, shows all his teeth. Waits
for Donovan to move.

                                        BACK TO SCENE

Donovan slowly hunkers down, extends his hand, fingers curled, hand a tight ball.
COOS to the dog in a high, soft voice.

                        DONOVAN
            Easy boy.

The dog sniffs the air. Cautiously steps forward, sniffs Donovan's hand. Licks
Donovan's hand. Okay with being petted.

Donovan reads the collar tag.

                    DONOVAN (CONT'D)
            Beg your pardon, Princess. Bet your owner is
            looking for you.

Princess wags her tail, sits, pants, content to lick Donovan's hand.

An elderly couple race up.

                        WOMAN
            Princess!   Darling!   Where'd you go?

Princess's ears perk up. She races to the couple who both bend to greet the dog.

                        MAN
            Thanks. She got off her leash.

The man quickly snaps the leash onto collar. The three walk away. Donovan
watches.

He walks a couple blocks, his gaze missing nothing. He stops seeing the house number on the building wall. He opens the wooden door.

EXT. COURTYARD

Shuts the door behind him. City sounds disappear.

Courtyard is a splendid garden, an oasis surrounded by city chaos, a water fountain in the middle of the garden.

Around perimeter is a walk. He follows it to left and stops at third door. Takes a key from his pocket and inserts into lock.

INT. APARTMENT

Enters, flicks light switch on wall. Light floods the room.

Wooden floors, minimum furniture. Couch, chair, table and chairs in the back, a small kitchen behind them.

He moves into--

INT. BEDROOM

--and turns on light. Plops bag on the bed, takes off jacket, and goes into--

INT. BATHROOM

--hangs jacket on knob. Turns on faucet, splashes water on face, towel dries, unbuttons shirt, takes it off.

INT. BEDROOM

Quickly empties bag, sets aside a dark box, opens drawers, puts clothing away. Shakes out a clean shirt and puts it on.

Finished, puts on jacket, pulls badge out of pocket, pulls wallet from his back pocket.

CLOSE ANGLE - WALLET

--as it opens. There's a definite impression where another badge once rested. The NEW ORLEANS BADGE is inserted.

BACK TO SCENE

Donovan snaps the wallet shut, returns to pocket. Reaches for black box, opens it.

Box of bullets, bulky-shaped dark cloth.

Reaches for the cloth, unwraps it. Gun. Loads it quickly, stuffing it in the back of his pants.

A pair of cuffs lie in the bottom of box. He starts to close the box, reconsiders, grabs the cuffs. Pockets them.

Grabs keys. Leaves.

EXT. BOURBON STREET - NIGHT

Evening celebration in full swing. Stores, bars and restaurants open. Area brightly lit, despite the late hour.

Street CROWDED, MUSIC BLARES from bars. PEOPLE LAUGH BAWDILY, a few PEDESTRIANS LURCH, obviously drunk.

CUT TO:

EXT. BOURBON STREET - LATER

Through a pizza parlor's glass window, Donovan gets up from a table where he's dined alone, leaving bills on the table.

Just outside the door frame, he pauses looking first one way, then another. He chooses a direction and starts walking.

INT. FRENCH QUARTER BAR

NOISY bar, smoke-filled. Mirror above the bar, runs the length of the bar.

Band plays CAJUN MUSIC. Couples dance, Jack among them.

Silky sits at bar, alone. Short skirt hiked up.

Drags on a cigarette, looks bored. Swings stool around, first toward the band. She and Jack exchange a quick glance.

Larry, and a few other men sit at a table nearby. She spins around 180 degrees.

Randy sits at the opposite end of the bar, where the bar curves around and meets the wall. Hunched over drink.

Silky's gaze lingers from table to table, eyeing different customers.

One man smiles drunkenly at her. She smiles back. The man's head drops to the table.

She turns back to her own drink. She picks it up, and with it almost to her mouth, mumbles.

CLOSE ANGLE - RANDY'S RIGHT SHOULDER AND HIS POV

A microphone cord comes out of his collar, leads to the earpiece nestled in his ear. Through his earphone--

> SILKY
> This tea sucks. I'm about to order a REAL
> drink.

She tosses back the tea, like a woman who's been without a drink for days.

Immediately, the bartender replaces the empty glass for a full one. She grimaces at him. The bartender winks at her.

Suddenly, her demeanor changes. She re-adjusts her bosom. Sits up straighter.

Randy turns his head toward the wall, coughing. He speaks softly.

> RANDY
> Sit tight, guys. The action's about to start. I
> swear the woman has radar.

BACK TO SCENE

The bar door opens. It's Donovan.

Silky raises her gaze to the mirror. They stare at each other.

Without lowering her gaze, she sticks her finger in her drink, sticks same finger in her mouth, drawing it out slowly, her lips making a tight "o" around it.

Donovan reluctantly tears his gaze away, scans the rest of the bar.

Randy huddles over his drink so he's not seen or recognized by Donovan.

Donovan lets the door shut behind him. Ignoring Silky, but well aware she's watching him, Donovan moves to the bar.

Straddles a bar stool, a couple seats away from Silky. Between Silky and Randy.

JOHN, young and who looks like he barely knows how to shave, plants himself on a stool on Silky's immediate other side.

Starts conversing with Silky. She glances at Donovan saucily, then turns her back to him, giving the new "customer" her undivided attention.

                         JOHN
                    (to bartender)
               Beer. Bud from tap.

                         BARTENDER
               Let's see some I.D.

John pulls his wallet from his back pocket, fishes out his I.D. and tosses it across the bar. The bartender scoops it up, glances at it, and smiles.

                         BARTENDER (CONT'D)
               Happy birthday, John.

                         SILKY
               John. Nice name. You alone?

                         JOHN
               As the night is long.

                         SILKY
               Poor baby.

                         JOHN
               Sure would be nice to celebrate with
               someone.

Donovan glares territorially at John, and John notices.

                         SILKY
               I could be that someone.

John slides his wallet off the bar.

Bartender puts a drink in front of John. Hands Silky a folded slip of paper. She doesn't open it.

                         SILKY (CONT'D)
               What's this?

                         BARTENDER
               From some man.

                         SILKY
               What man?

Bartender starts to point. Silky looks to where he's pointing. No one there.

                                BARTENDER
                        That's funny. He's gone now.

INSERT - PIECE OF PAPER

--as it's unfolded. Ivory colored.

"Queen of Hearts"

                                                        BACK TO SCENE

Silky frowns at it, flips it over. Nothing else. Frowns. Slips it down her skimpy top.
Turns to continue her conversation with John. He's gone.

Her head still turned, Donovan scoots over until he's seated next to Silky.

                                DONOVAN
                        Your friend left.

Silky startles and spins around. The surprise in her face changes to one of delight.

                            DONOVAN (CONT'D)
                        Must have thought you weren't interested.

                                SILKY
                        My, aren't we a big boy.

                                DONOVAN
                        Bet you say that to all the men.

                                SILKY
                        Only when they're naked.

Donovan grins slightly. A loud chuckle comes from a table behind her. A choking
sound comes from Randy. Silky looks past Donovan's shoulder. A man and a
woman, at a table behind her, have their heads together, sharing a joke or happy
moment.

CLOSE ANGLE - RANDY

He's mumbling again, pretending to grumble into his drink.

                                RANDY
                            Whatever happens, boys, stay back. Target's
                            okay. Cop, new in town. Couldn't have
                            planned this better myself.

                              SILKY
                How long y'all in town for?

                            DONOVAN
                Long enough.

He stares at Silky now, his gaze dropping to her chest, showing genuine interest.

                              SILKY
                Ever been to the mountains?

                            DONOVAN
                Now and then.

                              SILKY
                Where ya' from?

                            DONOVAN
                Does it matter?

                              SILKY
                Not really.

She takes an ice cube out of her drink and rubs it over her exposed breasts.

                            DONOVAN
                Too hot for you?

                              SILKY
                Could be even hotter for you... if you want.

                            DONOVAN
                I'd be foolish to say no when the lady is saying
                yes. How much?

                              SILKY
                How much you want?

                            DONOVAN
                All of you, baby, right down to your toes.

Silky turns, so she's facing him square, her legs fully between his, her knees just
inches from his crotch.

Her hands on his knees, she slides them up his thighs slowly. She smiles, looking him
up and down, taking in his measure fully.

                    SILKY
          Ah, well. Toes will cost you extra. Fifty per
          toe.

Donovan lifts an eyebrow.

                    DONOVAN
          Steep.

                    SILKY
          I'm worth it.

                    DONOVAN
          I bet you are. Too bad I won't have a chance
          to find out.

In a blink of an eye he's handcuffed one hand.

                    DONOVAN (CONT'D)
          You're under arrest. You have the right--

In the blink of another eyes, she's handcuffed the remaining cuff to his hand.

                    SILKY
          Think again, fucker. Okay, boys, take him!

Silky looks for Randy. He's mumbling in his drink, appearing to cough, sounds like a
laugh.

No one comes to her aid. Donovan stands up, jerking Silky along with him.

                    DONOVAN
          What's the matter, Toots?   No Prince
          Charming in sight?   Too bad. I'm taking you
          in.

Silky kicks him in the shin.

                    SILKY
          Pass that on to your friend.

Donovan growls, bends toward her, immediately retaliates and wraps his cuffed hand
behind her, forcing her cuffed hand to follow, lifting her up, pressing her to him.

                    DONOVAN
          What friend?

                    SILKY
          Don't toy with me. You're in cahoots with my
          cousin.

                    DONOVAN
          Lady, I don't know your cousin.

                    SILKY
          Be a nice guy and let me lose. I'm a cop.

                    DONOVAN
          Yeah, and my dick is purple.

                    SILKY
          It can be arranged.

Donovan sets her down and pulls her out--

EXT. BOURBON STREET

--into the street. Cat-calls and a few whistles are directed at Silky. Donovan arches an eyebrow at her.

                    DONOVAN
          Friends of yours?

Silky shrugs. She's pulled along. She glances behind her.

Randy and the others follow at a safe distance.

Silky trips. She can hardly keep up with Donovan's long strides and fast pace. She jerks their cuffed arms. She's back in character.

                    SILKY
          Either slow down, Sugar, or you'll have to
          carry me.

He moves even faster. She trips repeatedly.

                    SILKY (CONT'D)
          You're not only big, but you're stupid too.

                    DONOVAN
          Sticks and stones...

Silky, grins and sidles up next to him, rubbing her breast purposely against him, rubbing up and down.

Donovan looks down. She holds up their connected hands, shaking the cuffs.

SILKY

But leather and chains excite you. Come on,
what do you say we stop and check out your
long strapping leather.

EXT. POLICE PRECINCT

Donovan strides into the precinct. Silky is practically running now to keep up. Hoots
and hollers follow them through the precinct.

O.S. VOICE

Look! David's caught Goliath!

DESK SARGENT

David, don't you know your Bible stories?
You're supposed to stone him, between the
eyes, not chain him.

Silky grins widely, watching Donovan's cockiness dissipate.

SILKY

Catch of the day.

Donovan stops. He looks around in puzzlement. Behind him Randy and the other
boys, enter the door. A female uniformed officer walks past.

FEMALE OFFICER

Can I have him when you're done with him,
Silk?   I haven't had breakfast yet.

Donovan looks down at her.

DONOVAN

You're a cop.

SILKY

Told ya.

Donovan unlocks her cuff.

DONOVAN

Sorry.

SILKY

Fuck you.

She stalks off, leaving everyone. And their laughter. Takes off the heels while
walking, stomps up the stairs--

INT. POLICE REPORTING ROOM

--to her desk. Sits down, puts feet up, opens middle desk drawer, takes out a jaw breaker that's wrapped in clear plastic. Plops it in her mouth.

NEIL GUIDRY (now 27), good-looking, slim, sits at desk behind hers, their chairs normally back to back. Right now, his faces her.

> NEIL
> Geesh, Silky. Haven't you stopped that awful
> habit yet?

> SILKY
> What?   Talking to you?

> NEIL
> No. Talking while it looks like you've got a
> dick in your mouth.

> SILKY
> You're just jealous, Neil, that it's not yours.
> Oh that's right. I forgot. I'm not your type.

She winces, moves her shoulders, hunches them together, which compresses her breasts together. She digs out the slip of paper she stashed earlier, tosses it on top of her desk.

> NEIL
> Dad wants to see you first thing in the
> morning.

> SILKY
> It's my day off.

> NEIL
> You want detective or not?

He gets up and leaves. Silky stares after him.

Randy comes in as Neil goes out. She takes the jaw breaker out of her mouth, wraps it back up and returns it to its spot in her drawer.

Randy pulls the vacated chair out and sits so his back is to the rest of the room. He's obviously delighted with himself.

> RANDY
> Gotta admit, that was a good--

Silky raises a leg and plants her foot on his chair, between his legs, the heel of her foot catching the edge of seat. Randy looks down automatically.

                    RANDY (CONT'D)
          Christ, Silky. It almost looks like you're not
          wearing any--

She straightens her leg, pushes the chair and Randy with it across the room. The chair topples at the feet of Frisco, more muscled, who's doing paperwork at his desk.

He ignores Randy.

Silky gets up and walks past them both.

                    SILKY
          I'm not.

                    RANDY
                (looking after her)
          Jesus.

                    FRISCO
                (without looking up, talks while
                  writing)
          Shame, no one here can tame that kitten.

                    RANDY
          Wildcat, you mean.

Frisco looks up, just in time to see Silky disappear.

                    FRISCO
          She's asking for it.

INT. POLICE LOCKER ROOM - MORNING

Jack, at his locker, tucks his civilian shirt into his pants as Randy and Donovan come around the corner.

Randy shows Donovan his locker.

                    JACK
          Shame you're out of the running.

                    DONOVAN
          Didn't know I was in.

                    RANDY
          Big deal about being the first cop to get a
          bona fide kiss from Silky. Since breaking her
          engagement to Guidry junior, she's vowed
          never to get involved with a cop. Carries the
          biggest goddamn chip on her shoulder you've
          ever seen. She may be my cousin, but I'd love
          to see it knocked off.

                    DONOVAN
          What's the prize?

Jacks shuts his locker.

                    JACK
          Silky.

He grins.

                    JACK (CONT'D)
          Tough luck, old man. Thought you had a
          chance there last night before you cuffed her.

Jack looks him up and down the way Silky did the night before.

                    JACK (CONT'D)
          I think she could have liked you...

He winks at Donovan.

                    JACK (CONT'D)
          ...big boy.

Randy laughs. Jack walks away, adding--

                    JACK (CONT'D)
          Guidry wants to see you.

INT. GUIDRY'S OFFICE

Silky enters. Guidry stands at the window looking down.

GUIDRY'S POV.

On the street below, Neil crosses the street, stops two blonde, cute young women
who are walking together. Starts talking with them.

                                        BACK TO SCENE.

Guidry turns from window. Moves to desk, grabs a file. Tosses it to Silky.

She opens file. Several pictures of young girls, from 18 to mid-20s, all blonde, blue-eyed stare back at her. School photos.

                    GUIDRY
          We've got to get this guy.

Door OPENS again. Donovan enters.

                    GUIDRY (CONT'D)
          Good. You're both here. Silky, this is--

Silky looks up.

                    SILKY
          We've met.

                    DONOVAN
          Last night.

                    GUIDRY
          Great. Then we can get down to business.

He picks up second file. Hands it to Donovan. He thumbs through it.

                    GUIDRY (CONT'D)
          We've got a serial killer. A young woman
          found dead yesterday morning in the Garden
          District. Another one this morning. Mardi
          Gras officially starts in two weeks. I want this
          guy found before then. Donovan is your new
          partner.

                    SILKY
          Why him?   Randy's--

                    DONOVAN
          Don't do me any favors.

                    GUIDRY
          Randy's been reassigned.

Guidry turns and retreats back to the window. They've been dismissed.

Donovan and Silky move to leave.

                    GUIDRY (CONT'D)
          Silky wait.

Donovan hesitates, looks first at Guidry, then Silky and leaves, shutting door behind him.

Guidry turns around, facing her.

                    GUIDRY (CONT'D)
          Your ability to solve this case will determine
          whether you get the last homicide detective
          position or not.

Not happy. She doesn't respond.

INT. POLICE REPORTING ROOM

At her desk, Silky starts reading the first file. Donovan is seated across from her, their desks butted together. He's on the phone.

Randy sits at desk behind her, typing. Jack and Larry come to a halt near her desk.

                    LARRY
               (to Jack)
          You're a squirrel and you've hidden six ears of
          corn in a hollow log. Later you decide to
          move it out. You can only move three ears a
          day. How long does it take you to move the
          corn?

Donovan hangs up the phone. Neil perches on the edge of Randy's desk.

                    SILKY
          Six days.

                    LARRY
               (to Silky)
          How do you figure?

                    SILKY
          Besides an ear of corn, he's carrying his own
          two ears.

Donovan grabs the second folder from Silky's desk and opens it. Listens.

                    JACK
               (to Silky)
          And who was talking to you?   You need to be
          home tending to a loving husband.

RANDY

That leaves you out.

Jack walks off. Larry chuckles and picks up some papers out of the file she was
reading, glancing at it. Silky spins her chair around to face Randy.

SILKY

Stop doing that.

RANDY

What?

SILKY

I can take care of my own battles.

NEIL
(to Silky)
One of these days, someone's going to topple
your little glass house, Silk, my love.

SILKY

Unlike your windowless stone house?

Neil leaves. Randy extends his arms straight out toward Neil's back, his hand clasped
together as if he's holding a gun, a forefinger straight out like a gun and shoots.

RANDY

Bam!

He holsters his *gun*.

RANDY (CONT'D)
Someone needs to take him out. One bullet is
all it'll take. One. Through the heart. Bet he
wouldn't even feel it. He has no heart.

SILKY
Leave him alone.

LARRY
He dumped you.

SILKY
No, I dumped him.

RANDY
Why do you keep protecting him?

                              SILKY
               Scram.

Silky turns her chair back around, dismissing Randy. He sulks off. Donovan
watching her.

                             DONOVAN
               Popular, aren't we?

Frisco walks by.

                              FRISCO
               Regular queen of hearts.

Unnoticed by Larry, his very pregnant wife, PAT, waddles in. When Silky sees her,
Pat puts a finger to her lips, silencing her.

                              SILKY
               Ya', a regular Prom Queen.

                             DONOVAN
               What'd you do to piss them all off? Other
               than be a Miss-Know-It-All.

                              SILKY
               I grew breasts.

                              LARRY
               You can be my partner anytime, Silky. Breasts
               and all.

Pat is right behind Larry now.

                               PAT
               He's such a liar. Last thing he wants in a
               partner.

Larry jumps. Seeing his wife, he puts his arm around her, tucking her under his
shoulder.

                              LARRY
               But Sweetheart, you're my partner. And I love
               your breasts.

                               PAT
               If he weren't such a good cop, he'd be
               diagnosed as pathological.

She kisses her husband on the cheek and rubs her bulging stomach.

                    PAT (CONT'D)
I'm hoping his daughter--

                    LARRY
Son.

                    PAT
--will change his ways.

                    SILKY
How much longer?

                    PAT
Two weeks and I get to shoot this little pistol
out of this tired body.

Donovan stands.

                    DONOVAN
          (to Silky)
     Ready?

                                        CUT TO:

EXT. POLICE PRECINCT

Outside on the steps, Donovan and Silky meet JENNY and BECKY (15), with
braces.

                    SILKY
     Donovan, this is my sister-in-law, Jenny, and
     my favorite niece, Becky.

                    JENNY
     Ex sister-in-law. I was married to her brother,
     Jason. I remarried.

Donovan greets Jenny, then Becky.

                    DONOVAN
     You and your aunt look a lot alike.

                    BECKY
We're twins.

Guidry comes out of the building, greeting Jenny and Becky.

                              BECKY (CONT'D)
                    We came to show Silky my new braces.

                              GUIDRY
                    I thought there was something different about
                    you. Pretty as a picture.

He pinches her cheek, waves to them all, and leaves.

                              BECKY
                    You coming Sunday to the family dinner?

                              SILKY
                    Don't I always?

                              JENNY
                         (laughing, to Donovan)
                    Even though she'd rather not.

EXT. CRIME SCENE - ST. LOUIS #1 CEMETERY - LATER

Police cars block the street. Yellow police tape circles around a number of the above
ground burial sites, a covered body in the center.

Tourists stand at the perimeter of the tape, ever curious. Policemen, Larry, and Jack
look for clues in the area. Donovan lifts the tape, Silky and he move under it, into
the crime arena.

Silky picks up a loose piece of brick and marks an "X" on the wall of one of the
tombs.

                              DONOVAN
                    What'd you do that for?

                              SILKY
                    Good luck.

CLOSE ANGLE - TOMB

"Marie Laveau"

                                                       BACK TO SCENE

                              DONOVAN
                    Who's she?

                              SILKY
              The grand dame of voodoo queens, self-
              appointed Pope of Voodoo in the 1830s.

                             DONOVAN
              You believe in that shit?

Two cops who overhear look at each other. Donovan notices.

                              JACK
              You will.

                             LARRY
              You will.

                              SILKY
              You live here long enough, you will.

Silky moves to the body, lifts up a corner of the cloth, lets it drop back down.
Coroner is nearby.

                          SILKY (CONT'D)
              What have we got?

                            CORONER
              Caucasian female, blonde, pretty, about 23,
              24. She was raped and her heart's missing.
              About 4 a.m., I'd say.

                             DONOVAN
              Geezus.

SILKY'S POV on a small white piece of paper jammed up against one of the graves
fluttering in the slight breeze, the color blending in well with the wall of the ivory
concrete grave.

She goes, pulling on a glove, picks it up. Handles just an edge.

Jack is there with a clear plastic bag and she drops the paper in it. Jack holds it up so
they can have a better look at it. Donovan is now behind Silky, looking too.

CLOSEUP - PAPER

"FOR WANT OF A NAIL"

                                                      BACK TO SCENE

                              JACK
                    What does it mean?

                            DONOVAN
                    Probably just someone's garbage blowing
                    around.

                             SILKY
                    Possibly. Then again maybe not.

                              JACK
                    Don't see how Guidry connects these two
                    crimes. Looks unrelated to me.

                             SILKY
                    They're related somehow. Carl's instincts are
                    the best in the precinct.

She points to a small rusty red marking located on the grave wall just above where
the note was. She looks around and spots the photographer, TONY.

                         SILKY (CONT'D)
                    Tony, I want some pictures of that.

Donovan squats down for a closer look.

A huge big spider crawls across the marking. Startled, Donovan yelps, backs up,
nearly falling on his butt, staring at the creature.

                         SILKY (CONT'D)
                    Amazing how the smallest things can bring a
                    giant to his knees...or butt.

Donovan gets up, dusts himself off.

                         SILKY (CONT'D)
                    You'll love where we're going next.

On her way to the car, to a nearby cop--

                         SILKY (CONT'D)
                    Tell the boys to hurry up and get that body
                    out of here. Can't keep the tourists from
                    Marie too long.

EXT. BOURBON STREET - HOUSE OF VOODOO - DAY

Streets are nearly deserted compared to the night before.

Tourists going in and out of stores, carrying shopping bags rather than drinks. Demeanor is quiet, more polite.

INT. HOUSE OF VOODOO

Dark, eerie, sinister looking. Black candles, skulls, African statues and masks, jars of colored powder, snakes, Damballah everywhere.

Donovan and Silky enter. They're alone in the store.

                    DONOVAN
          Remind me later. I need a booster tetanus
          shot.

BANJO comes from the back room. Hair shaven close to scalp. He's huge, black, in his 50s.

Dressed in black, a shirt with sleeves torn off reveal oversized muscles.

His expression, one of complete joy at seeing Silky, doesn't match the surroundings. Silky opens her mouth to speak, but Banjo holds up his hands, his demeanor changing to one of thought.

Silky stands still. Donovan frowns.

Banjo appears to be listening to something, his eyes squinting as he peers at Silky.

                    BANJO
          This thing you're involved in-- follow your
          instincts.
                    (to Donovan)
          Learn to love them. They're your friends. The
          ones with eight.

                    DONOVAN
                    (whispering to Silky)
          Who?

                    SILKY
          Spiders.

                    DONOVAN
          Never.

Instantly, the moment, the mood is gone. Banjo's big welcoming smile is back. He goes to hug Silky, but then at the last minute draws back.

                              BANJO
            You haven't been mad at ole Banjo have you?
            You've been away too long.

She punches him affectionately in the chest. As effective as a pebble hitting a whale.
They embrace.

                              SILKY
            I'd like you to meet my new partner, Donovan
            O'Roarke.

They shake hands.

                              BANJO
            You don't like our store.

                             DONOVAN
            Too dark for me.

                              BANJO
            Darkness is in the heart of the beholder.

Silky goes to the counter, picks up a pencil and turns over the receipt pad. She
quickly sketches the drawing she saw earlier on Marie's tomb. She holds the pad out
to Banjo.

                              SILKY
            What do you know of this?

Banjo looks at it, his eyes troubled as he looks back at her.

                              BANJO
            You found this near a dead one?

                              SILKY
            Yes.

                              BANJO
            I've not seen this for a long time. Very long
            time. Her heart gone?

Silky nods.

                              SILKY
            I think it was written in blood. Not brick like
            all the other signs in the cemetery.

                    BANJO
          Be careful. If it is what I think, this person
          plays for keeps.

                    DONOVAN
          That's all you can tell us?

                    BANJO
          Right now, that's all I know.

His look becomes thoughtful.

                    BANJO (CONT'D)
               (to Silky)
          You already know what's going to happen.
          You haven't learned to trust yourself
          completely yet.

                    SILKY
          Thanks, Banjo. You've been a help.

Silky and Donovan turn to leave.

                    BANJO
          Goliath!

They look back.

                    BANJO (CONT'D)
               (to Donovan)
          It wasn't your fault.

EXT. VOODOO MUSEUM

                    SILKY
          What did he mean, not your fault?

                    DONOVAN
          You tell me.
               (beat)
          He knew the heart was missing. That makes
          him a prime suspect.

                    SILKY
          You're not in New York anymore. He's not a
          suspect.

                    DONOVAN
          Where'd your friend study at? Fright U
          Academy?   All we needed in there was some
          thunder and lightning.

Thunder.

Donovan looks up at the sky in disbelief.

Heavy downpour.

EXT. FRENCH QUARTER - RESTAURANT

They join a group of people standing under the canopy trying to escape the rain,
hugging the building.

Silky shakes the front of her soaking wet blouse away from her skin. Donovan runs a
hand through his hair, to no good.

                    DONOVAN
          Does it always rain like this?

                    SILKY
          Always. You'll get used to it.

They squeeze through the throng of people standing in the open doorway into--

INT. RESTAURANT

--where the host greets Silky by name and shows them to a window table.

                    SILKY
          I take it you've never been to N'awlins before?

                    DONOVAN
          No.

                    SILKY
          Like hot food?

                    DONOVAN
          Doesn't any red-blooded American man? I'm
          from New York remember. You Southerners
          don't have the market on heat.

                    SILKY
          Let me order.

MINUTES LATER--

The waitress sets their plates in front of them. Immediately, Silky picks up the Tabasco Sauce and dumps quite a bit of it over her food. Donovan watches.

                         DONOVAN
          That mild?

                         SILKY
          Yup.

She sets the bottle down, he picks it up and splashes a good bit over his food. She's already eating, with no reaction whatsoever to the *heat*.

He takes a huge forkful of food. Instantly, he grabs his water, gulps it down, grabs hers, gulps it down.

                         DONOVAN
               (gasping)
          You said it was mild!

                         SILKY
               (grinning)
          It is, for a native.

She continues eating. Their water gone, he grabs a pitcher of water off the next table, startling the patrons. They back away from him as he gulps it down.

                         SILKY (CONT'D)
          Don't mind him. He just returned from the
          desert.

                                                  CUT TO:

INT. CAR - AFTERNOON

Silky drives. Donovan holds radio microphone in his hand.

VOICE O.S.

--another body. Bonard farm.

EXT. BONARD FARM

A small, unpainted farm house with tin roof.

A few chickens scratch at bare ground

Nearby an equally small, unpainted barn.

Various parts of rusty machinery are scattered like seeds in field and barnyard.

Two police cars in driveway. A stooped old man, BONARD, in his 70s, talks with Randy. Larry looks around.

                    BONARD
          I'm just a retired vet. Only shoe horses
          anymore. Found her when I came out to
          gather some eggs for dinner.

Donovan and Silky examine the body. Young woman, blonde, early 20s, pretty. No shoes. Jeans and a jacket.

Donovan frowns, hunkers down looking at her feet, particularly the soles.

                    DONOVAN
          Take a look at this.

Silky and Larry move down for a closer look.

CLOSE ANGLE - SOLES OF FEET

--which are dirty as if she's been barefoot. Near the heel of one foot is something else. Faint bruising.

                                        BACK TO SCENE

                    DONOVAN
          Puncture wounds.

                    LARRY
          Probably stepped on something. Gotta be
          nails around here.

                    DONOVAN
          Those are bite wounds.

                    SILKY
          Snake?

                    LARRY
          What are you?   A former Boy Scout?

                    DONOVAN
              Eagle Scout. Anyone got a glove?

Larry hands him a pair of gloves. Donovan puts them on and starts checking the
girl's pockets. He pulls out a piece of paper.

CLOSEUP - PAPER

"And the cow jumped"

                                              BACK TO SCENE

                    SILKY
                (to Donovan)
              Over the moon.

                    DONOVAN
              What?

                    SILKY
              The cow jumped over the moon. It's a nursery
              rhyme. Hey Diddle, Diddle.

                                              CUT TO:

INT. LIBRARY

At the front desk, Silky and Donovan check out a pile of library books.

EXT. LIBRARY PARKING LOT

Silky and Donovan walk down the steps. Donovan carries most of the books.

                    DONOVAN
              I can't ever remember checking out a book of
              rhymes, let alone one of nursery rhymes.

                    SILKY
              Really? I used to read them to Becky all the
              time. So how long has it been since you were
              even in a library?

                    DONOVAN
              High school.

SILKY
And it was... let me guess... a biography on
Abraham Lincoln. You had to do a report on
an American President.

Donovan stops in his tracks and stares at her, amazed.

DONOVAN
What are you, clairvoyant?

Silky chuckles.

SILKY
Every senior has to write a term paper if
they're going to college. You're a police
officer. You went to college. You had to do
the paper. What's easier than researching a
President. What President has oodles of
information?   Kennedy, Washington,
Lincoln. You look like a Lincoln man.

DONOVAN
And... you did Kennedy.

SILKY
How do you figure?

DONOVAN
He was a lady's man. You look like the
vulnerable type.

SILKY
I was never vulnerable.

DONOVAN
Okay, let me rephrase that. Gullible.

SILKY
Only for a great looking man.

His eyebrows go up.

SILKY (CONT'D)
Non-cop.

At the same time, they both notice a male figure, his back to them, trying to jimmy
open a car door.

SILKY (CONT'D)
(in a low voice)
In broad daylight.

She reaches for her gun. Donovan reaches for his.

                                        CUT TO:

CLOSE ANGLE - THIEF

--as he fails to catch the lock. He tries again, this time triumphant. He opens the
door.

SILKY (V.O.)
Police! Freeze!

Thief pulls out a gun, spins, finds Silky and Donovan, both prepared to shoot,
separated by enough distance that he has to choose one or the other to point his gun
at.

He aims first at one, then the other, switching back and forth.

Deadly intent that first appeared on his face, turns to indecision.

DONOVAN
You can't take us both out. Either drop it or
choose.

The thief hesitates, drops the gun, raises both hands in the air.

SILKY
On your knees.

The thief drops.

DONOVAN
Flat on the ground, legs and arms spread out.

The thief complies. Silky cuffs one hand, then cuffs him to the car. Donovan
holsters his cuff, runs a hand through his hair and paces.

She watches him while calling in, using her shoulder mike. She walks toward
Donovan.

THIEF
Hey, you can't leave me here like this!

When she's caught up to Donovan, Silky reaches out, stops him. He turns.

                    SILKY
This is connected to the New York shooting,
isn't it?

                    DONOVAN
No.

                    SILKY
Liar. Your body language says otherwise. It's
the first time you've had to pull out your gun
since, isn't it? I read the papers, you know.

                    DONOVAN
Ever shoot the wrong person?

                    SILKY
No. I'm an excellent shot.

                    DONOVAN
I thought I was too.

A police car with lights pulls up.

INT. SILKY'S APARTMENT - EVENING

Large pizza box is open, one piece remaining. Books are spread around, some open,
some not.

Donovan sits on the couch, slugging back the last of a beer. He plops the empty can
on the coffee table.

Silky sits on the floor on the opposite side of the table, shoves the last bit of her slice
in her mouth, wipes her mouth on a napkin. Balls it up, tosses it into the pizza box.

                    SILKY
Last piece is yours.

                    DONOVAN
Save it for breakfast.

Silky jumps up, gathers boxes, other food paraphernalia, takes it all into kitchen.
Returns with two cans of soda. Hands one to Donovan.

                    SILKY
That was the last of the beer.

DONOVAN
Just as well. One more and I'll be in a stupor.
Between that and these damn lullabies.

He sets the soda down unopened, closes a book with a thump, gets up, strolls to
window, looks out.

DONOVAN (CONT'D)
Why nursery rhymes?

SILKY
He's trying to be cute.

DONOVAN
You say he. Why not she?

SILKY
Rape's involved. Torture. Women aren't
messy like that. Plus, it's a serial killer. Men
tend to be the serial killers.

Donovan stares at her. She stares back.

Beat.

Obvious attraction.

Finally, Donovan sighs, runs his hand through his hair, rubs the back of neck.

DONOVAN
We can read these books all night and come
up with nothing.

SILKY
How are you with computers?

She slips her gun holster on and puts on her jacket. Donovan does likewise.

DONOVAN
I get by.

SILKY
Great. I hate them.

Donovan opens her door. He stops abruptly. Keeps her from moving forward.
Takes out his gun, finger on the trigger, looks both ways, steps over the threshold.

DONOVAN'S POV

--as he looks both ways. Empty hall. All doors closed.

Complete silence. No footsteps, no doors closing.

Donovan holsters his gun. He kneels to get a closer look at the threshold. A mixture of red and black powder, very fine, in a pile. He fingers it and sniffs. He coughs.

> SILKY
> It's gun powder and red pepper. A voodoo
> conjuration. A curse.

> DONOVAN
> This kind of thing happen often?

> SILKY
> I'm a cop. It's not the first time. I doubt it'll
> be the last.

> DONOVAN
> You're not concerned?

> SILKY
> If I worried every time someone threatened
> me, I'd never open my door.

Silky steps back into the apartment, reaches into a jar of dimes. Pulls one out. Shoves it into a crack in the door frame.

Donovan notices multiple dimes in the door frame.

> DONOVAN
> Don't tell me. It's good luck.

> SILKY
> Counter-acts the curse. It's as good as a bullet
> proof vest.

> DONOVAN
> Seriously. That's nonsense.

Beat.

> DONOVAN (CONT'D)
> That many? You *are* popular.

INT. POLICE PRECINCT

Donovan sits in front of the computer at his desk. Silky stands behind him, watching. He does a search for nursery rhymes.

> DONOVAN
> Real simple.

> SILKY
> Only to a computer nerd.

> DONOVAN
> Guilty as charged.

He taps the keys faster than anyone she's ever seen. She's impressed.

While Donovan punches keys, she picks up file marked *Anne Walker*. Opens file. Examines a photo of dead girl under bushes in Garden District.

Second picture is close up of the chain and silver bell around her neck.

> SILKY
> Do a search for silver bell.

He types in the words. He grabs a pencil off his desk, a scrap of paper off of hers.

He looks at the scrap, frowns, then looks startled.

He straightens, grabs the files on her desk, files regarding their cases.

> SILKY (CONT'D)
> What is it?

Donovan hands her the scrap. She looks at it.

> SILKY (CONT'D)
> *Queen of hearts.* So what? From each file, he
> pulls out a piece of paper.

> DONOVAN
> Look at the handwriting.

Silky does.

CLOSE ANGLE - NOTES

The handwriting is same.

BACK TO SCENE

                    DONOVAN
          The paper's the same too. Where'd it come
          from?

He's indicating the *Queen of Hearts* paper.

Silky looks at him. For the first time, there's a kink in her hard-boiled armor.

                    SILKY
          I got it the night we met. At the bar. The
          bartender said it came from a man. I never
          saw him.

Donovan types again. Computer screen changes.

CLOSE ANGLE - COMPUTER SCREEN

Nursery rhyme "Queen of Hearts" displayed.

                                        BACK TO SCENE

Donovan hits another key, printer starts.

                                        CUT TO:

Printer finished, Donovan grabs the print-out, adding it to the pile already in Silky's hands.

                    DONOVAN
          That's all of them.

Silky yawns. Donovan takes the papers from her.

                    DONOVAN (CONT'D)
          Let's call it a night. It's been a long day.

                    SILKY
          I have a feeling tomorrow's going to be even
          longer.

INT. SILKY'S BEDROOM - LATE NIGHT

Room is dark. Window open, the curtain lifts at the slightest breeze

Silky, in bed, asleep, moans.

From a distance is the muffled SOUND of CHURCH BELLS CHIMING THE HOUR.

SILKY'S DREAM

Blurry background. Appears church-like with stained glass.

Small altar, table top covered with black cloth. Burning candles.

Room is dark, lost in shadows. She's young, about 7. She stands at the alter, looking down at her shoes.

                    MALE VOICE (O.S.)
          I'll be Jack and you'll be Jill.

Her head remains bent.

                    SILKY
               (whispering)
          No.

                    MALE VOICE (O.S.)
               (soft, drawn out)
          Silky.

She hunches over, her hands clenched together.

                    SILKY
               (scared)
          Noooo.

                    MALE VOICE (O.S.)
          Come here, Silky.

INT. SILKY'S BEDROOM

Silky jerks to sitting position, eyes wide open, terror on her face.

                    SILKY
          Noooooooooo!

She's awake now. She's shaken. She runs a hand through her hair. She frowns, looks around the room as if searching for a bogey man.

The phone RINGS. She jumps, snatches it.

                    SILKY (CONT'D)
          David here.

She listens.

                              SILKY (CONT'D)
          Geezus.
                    (beat)
          I'll be right there.

She throws off the covers, grabs her jeans.

EXT. CRIME SCENE - MOON WALK - NIGHT

An almost full moon rises in the b.g., against the Mississippi River. A barge
silhouetted against the moon.

Near the river's edge, on the rocks, is a woman's body. Young. Dressed, blood thick
on her chest. She's laid out, legs together, arms at her side, eyes closed.

White markings, on the rocks, extend out from the body. Looks eerie in moonlight.

Looking down at her from the grassy edge above is Silky. Donovan joins her.

                              SILKY
          One bullet. Through the heart. Exit wound in
          the back. Heart's gone.

Silky hands him a piece of paper, encased in a plastic bag. Donovan reads the note.

                              DONOVAN
          Ladybird.

He looks at Silky, puzzled.

                              SILKY
          I lay odds we'll find it in a nursery rhyme.

Neil joins them. Looks over the edge.

                              NEIL
          Looks like a fucking sacrifice.

Donovan frowns.

                              DONOVAN
          What are you doing here?

                              NEIL
          I was with Tony.

He indicates the police photographer down below taking snapshots.

NEIL (CONT'D)
We were playing poker when the call came in.
Had a straight flush. Best hand I've had all
night.

He walks away, gets in his car, leaves.

INT. POLICE PRECINCT - CONFERENCE ROOM - DAY

Donovan and Silky in corner of room. It's obvious they've been up all night. Files
scattered on table.

They stand, facing a white board: each of the victims are in a row on the left side.
Rows and columns extend out from the pictures.

Different columns show: where body discovered, age, name, how killed, clues found
with body, what notes said, the nursery rhymes they've connected the notes to.

Also, a picture of the drawing on Marie's grave. Both Donovan and Silky lean against
table studying the board, arms crossed.

DONOVAN
Other than the nursery rhymes, I don't see
anything else in common here.

SILKY
They're all in the same age group. Late teens,
early- to mid-twenties.

DONOVAN
There's got to be something more.

They both continue staring at the board. Silky gets up and paces.

SILKY
The victims are listed in order of their death.
(beat)
Wait a minute. I got that note after Anne's
death but before Michelle's.

Silky goes to the board, draws a line under Anne Walkers's row, inserts a new row.

Under the column "Note," she writes: Queen of Hearts.

Donovan watches. Suddenly, he's alert, his body stiffens.

Slowly, he straightens, takes a step toward the board.

                    DONOVAN
          The victim after your note of Queen of
          Hearts note had her heart ripped out.

                    SILKY
          The note found on Michelle said "for want of
          a nail" and the next victim had two puncture
          wounds.

                    DONOVAN
          Is the autopsy report back yet?

                    SILKY
          No.

                    DONOVAN
          The cow jumped--

                    SILKY
          Over the moon. Moon walk.

                    DONOVAN
          And now Ladybird. Ladybird, ladybird, fly
          away home...

EXT. NEW ORLEANS INTERNATIONAL AIRPORT - DAY

Silky and Donovan drive up, exit the car. Passengers, coming and going, rush past
them.

Usual travel scene of people hugging. Porters take luggage at the curb. Cars and
buses come and go. Bedlam.

                    DONOVAN
          Such a huge airport for such a small ladybug.

Silky turns to Donovan.

                    SILKY
          What'd you say?

                                                        CUT TO:

EXT. CAR

Turns off of I-10.

CLOSEUP - SIGN

"Lakefront Airport"

BACK TO SCENE

A car passes, from the opposite direction.

Frisco driving, face thunderous. Doesn't notice Silky and Donovan.

Silky's gaze follows the car.

> SILKY
> That looked like Frisco.

EXT. LAKEFRONT AIRPORT

They pull up to the entrance, curb car, exit.

Across the drive, is a small parking lot, half-filled.

One passenger with suitcase and luggage comes out of the airport.

No planes take off. A plane sits out behind the small building.

INT. LAKEFRONT AIRPORT

Silky goes up the first airport personnel she sees, shows badge.

Donovan disappears into men's bathroom.

Clerk shakes his head no. Silky heads for the *Ladies* bathroom. Before she goes in, Donovan comes out of men's restroom.

> DONOVAN
> Nothing.

INT. LADIES RESTROOM

Silky checks all the stalls. Looks everywhere. Behind the seats, in wastebaskets.

Wrinkles her nose, checks the rest of the bathroom, finds nothing.

INT. LAKEFRONT AIRPORT

She meets Donovan who's come from the baggage area.

                    DONOVAN
          Nothing.

Together they head toward the boarding gates.

Along the way, they check behind chairs, trash cans, looking in the cans.

In the boarding area, they check everything. Finally, behind a potted plant, Donovan
stops.

                    DONOVAN (CONT'D)
          Over here.

Silky joins Donovan.

CLOSE ANGLE - BONES

In a neat pile, with a note propped next to it.

The note: "FE, FI, FO, FUM, EVEN EXCHANGE"

                                        BACK TO SCENE

                    DONOVAN
          Another clue.

                    SILKY
          At least it's not another victim. Looks like
          chicken bones.

                    DONOVAN
          For now. If we don't figure out this clue, there
          could be another body sooner than we'd like.

INT. LAKEFRONT AIRPORT

Donovan takes a picture. Silky picks up the bones with her hand in a plastic bag and
inserts them into another bag.

EXT. LAKEFRONT AIRPORT

Donovan and Silky walk to the car.

                    DONOVAN
              (in a deep booming voice
               imitating a giant)
          Fe, fi, fo, fum. I smell the blood of an
          Englishman.

Silky frowns, is slower than Donovan to get into the car.

Donovan starts the car and they pull away from the terminal.

EXT. CAR

Traveling on the road away from the airport.

INT. CAR

Silky looks at the note in her hand, now encased in a plastic bag, bones in a second bag.

                    DONOVAN
          What does that pile represent?

                    SILKY
          Other than four dead chickens?

                    DONOVAN
          Four?

                    SILKY
          I can reassemble the pile without a picture.

Donovan looks at her sharply.

                    DONOVAN
          Voodoo?

She nods.

                    SILKY
          He's evil.
              (beat)
          Misguided certainly.

                    DONOVAN
          He's a fucking murderer!

SILKY

Yes, he's a murderer. But voodoo isn't evil.
It's a viable religion.

DONOVAN

Yeah, just like the Pope.

SILKY

Exactly.

DONOVAN

No way can you convince me that voodoo is
good.

SILKY

The music and dance recognize the dead.
Masks honor the deities, animals, and Mother
Nature.

DONOVAN

Trappings. It's all trappings.

SILKY

So are robes, candles, altar boys, cathedrals,
monster organs. All religions have rituals.
Voodoo is no different.

DONOVAN

Like red pepper and black powder on your
doorstep.

SILKY

Any ritual can be twisted and contorted to
represent evil. Evil gets publicized, goodness
doesn't. Do you believe in Halloween?

DONOVAN

That's not the same thing at all.

SILKY

It is if you know the holiday originated as a
celebration to honor The Saints.

DONOVAN

Seriously?

SILKY

Obviously, we need to make another trip to
the library for your ed-u-ca-tion.

Silky stares ahead.

SILKY'S DREAM

The same background as before. Altar. Stained glass. Burning candles. She's still 7. Her eyes shut tight, her hands clenched.

                         MALE VOICE (O.S.)
               Tell me the lesson you've learned, Silky.

Her voice is a mere whisper.

                         YOUNG SILKY
               It's better to give than receive. His hand
               comes into view. It's barely identifiable as
               most of it is covered by the long sleeve of a
               black robe.

A finger under her chin, he tilts her head up. She continues to look down. One lone tear trickles down her cheek. But then she looks up and her eyes show hatred and fear.

                         MALE VOICE (O.S.)
                    (chuckling)
               You must learn to control your anger, my
               dear. It doesn't become you.

                                             DREAM ENDS

                         DONOVAN
               Silky?

She looks at him, as if coming out of a fog. One lone tear tracks its way across her cheek, exactly as in her dream.

The car is parked alongside the road. Lake Ponchartrain on their right. Engine turned off. Donovan is twisted in his seat, facing her.

                         DONOVAN (CONT'D)
               What is it?

Silky blinks several times, looks around, frowns.

                         SILKY
               Why did we stop?

                         DONOVAN
               Where were you?

She stares out the window again, but only for a second. With her hands she wipes at her eyes and her face as if to wipe away the exhaustion. She turns back to Donovan, her expression back to normal.

                    SILKY
          Must have dozed off. Comes with the
          territory, you know that.
                    (beat)
          Why N'awlins?   Why did you pick here to
          start over?

Now she's staring at him, her gaze intense and just as pointed as her question.

Donovan restarts the car.

                    DONOVAN
          Why not?   It's warm, has a party atmosphere.

                    SILKY
          And a place where you can hide your sorrow.
          So, what are you hiding? It must have been
          horrible for you. Finding you'd killed the
          victim instead of the kidnapper.

His jaw tightens.

                    DONOVAN
          It was.
                    (beat)
          Guidry gave me an opportunity too good to
          pass up.

                    SILKY
          Which was?

                    DONOVAN
          Homicide detective.

INT. POLICE PRECINCT - GUIDRY'S OFFICE - DAY

Guidry is at his desk, reading a report.

Silky, her gaze intense, enters the room, pushes the door shut with one hand not caring that it rattles the glass. Guidry looks up. He closes the report, leans back in his chair.

                    GUIDRY
          Let me guess. You're unhappy.

Silky leans against the door.

                    SILKY
          You offered my position to Donovan.

                    GUIDRY
          Your position?   Presumptuous, aren't we?

Silky runs her hand through her hair, frustrated.

                    SILKY
          You promised me.

                    GUIDRY
          That's not true.

                    SILKY
          Then you owe me. I'm the best you've got and
          you know it. I'm tired of being in vice.

                    GUIDRY
          Then bring me something. Anything. Get City
          Hall off my neck.

INT. POLICE PRECINCT

Donovan at the vendor machines, changing dollar bill for coins. He deposits two
coins. Nothing happens. He kicks the machine.

Frisco walks by.

                    DONOVAN
          It's a conspiracy.

Frisco stops, concentrates on the machine, almost hugging it as he rubs both hands
along the sides of the machine. Then with just the tip of a finger, he taps twice above
the coin entry. A can of soda pops out.

                    FRISCO
          Talk nice to it. Like a woman. It'll reward you
          every time.

                    DONOVAN
          Is that why you were out near Lakefront this
          afternoon?

Frisco glares at him.

                    DONOVAN (CONT'D)
            (continuing)
        Silk and I saw you.

                    FRISCO
        A mistake I won't make with that bitch again.
        Had an afternoon away from her snoopy
        husband tailing her and what does she do? I
        find her balling some cracker.

Frisco leaves. Donovan stares after him, grabs the can, then looks at it thoughtfully.
He puts the other two coins in the machine. He mimics Frisco's movement when the
can doesn't drop.

It drops. Coroner walks up.

                    CORONER
        Don't think about it too long. Just reading the
        label of ingredients could kill ya'.

He indicates the can in the machine.

                    CORONER (CONT'D)
        Yours?

                    DONOVAN
        Nope. Yours.
            (beat)
        Not enough conversation at your office?

Coroner grabs it and pops it open.

                    CORONER
        Yeah, nothing but a bunch of stiffs down
        there. No fun at all-- they don't gossip.

He hands Donovan a file folder.

                    CORONER (CONT'D)
        Results of the last two victims. Donovan flips
        through it.

                    DONOVAN
        What'd you find out?

                    CORONER
        Those puncture wounds were from a bat.

                              DONOVAN
                 Bats don't bite humans unless provoked.

Coroner looks at him.

                         DONOVAN (CONT'D)
                 NatGeo channel.

Larry approaches the vending machine, inserts his coin. A can rattles down the chute
into the bin. Larry picks it up.

                              CORONER
                 What's even stranger is it's a vampire bat,
                 found only in Central and South America.

                              LARRY
                 Sounds like another case.

                              DONOVAN
                 When?

                              LARRY
                 Few years back. Five maybe.

INT. POLICE REPORTING ROOM

Donovan at the computer, fingers flying across keyboard. He waits, peers intently at
screen. Hits print button. Printer starts printing out a list.

INT. POLICE PRECINCT - FILES DEPARTMENT

Donovan hands the printed list to the clerk.

                              DONOVAN
                 I'd like these files.

The clerk moves down one of many rows, stopping, pulls down one file, moves on,
pulls another.

INT. POLICE PRECINCT - CONFERENCE ROOM

Silky enters the room, finds Donovan pouring over files. She comes up behind him.

INSERT - BLACK AND WHITE PHOTO

--of Jessica, dead, laying in a tangle of pine needles and debris, a dark stain covering the left portion of her chest.

> DONOVAN
> Jessica Horton. Died fifteen years ago. One bullet through the heart. Raped. Case still open.

Silky picks up the file.

> SILKY
> So what are you doing with her?

> DONOVAN
> I pulled all the files of unsolved crimes involving young women. I found a dozen, three that may be linked to our killer.

She sits down.

> SILKY
> That makes seven, then.

> DONOVAN
> And there's probably more.

She looks at the pictures from the three new files.

> SILKY
> Wait a minute. These girls are much younger.

> DONOVAN
> Put them in order chronologically.

Silky turns to the blackboard.

> SILKY
> My god. It's almost as if we're watching her age.

> DONOVAN
> That's the first similarity. There's more.

He tacks up the new pictures, up above the others.

> SILKY
> They're all blonde.

                    DONOVAN
          And blue-eyed.

Silky picks up Jessica's file again, flipping through the papers.

                    SILKY
          This file is thinner than the others.

Her expression shows surprise.

                    SILKY (CONT'D)
          These are Jason's notes.

                    DONOVAN
          Jason?

                    SILKY
          My brother. Killed in a shoot-out when I was
          ten.

                    DONOVAN
          I'm sorry.
                    (beat)

                    DONOVAN (CONT'D)
          Is there a relative of yours that isn't a cop?

                    SILKY
          Just the women. Mom hates that I'm a cop. A
          repeated topic at family dinners.

INT. GUIDRY'S OFFICE

Guidry stands at the window, looking out, lost in thought.

Silky knocks on the door. Guidry turns, sees her, signals for her to come in. He
moves to his chair.

                    SILKY
          Do you remember the last case Jason worked
          on?

                    GUIDRY
          Vaguely.
                    (beat)
          She was young. Shot through the heart if I
          remember right.

                    SILKY
          What happened?

                    GUIDRY
          Occurred same time as your dad and Jason...
          Case got passed on after that. I got promoted.
          So many changes...

Long beat.

                    SILKY
          The file's thin. Too thin.

                    GUIDRY
          Your father might remember more. Jason may
          have talked with him.

INT. POLICE REPORTING ROOM

Silky sees Larry at his desk. She rests against the edge of his desk. Watches him work at the computer.

He ignores her.

                    SILKY
          What do you remember of your first case?

                    LARRY
          Nothing. Don't want to remember.

                    SILKY
          Who got reassigned to--

                    LARRY
          I don't know. Don't want to talk about it. I
          want to forget that day, that case.

Silky stands.

                    SILKY
          What'samatter?   Fight with the wife?

He ignores her. She walks away. For the first time, he stops typing. He glares at her back.

INT. POLICE PRECINCT - CONFERENCE ROOM

Silky rejoins Donovan.

                    SILKY
          Anything?

                    DONOVAN
          Only that nursery rhymes aren't for kids. Do
          you realize how much death there are in these
          things?

She indicates the pictures on the blackboard.

                    SILKY
          Bet they could tell you a lot about it.

She spots a large envelop on the table.

                    DONOVAN
          Jessica's personal belongings.

She opens it and turns it upside-down. Out spills red pants and a red & white striped
shirt, and a bracelet. Clothes are dirty, blood stained. Donovan picks up the bracelet,
runs his finger over the two snakes.

                    SILKY
          Damballah and his mate Aia-Wedo.

Silky spots a small pocket on the shirt. Gingerly, she pulls out an old, note.

Ivory colored.

Her gaze meets Donovan's.

INT. BAR - DUSK

Where Silky and Donovan first met. A few customers.

Same bartender that was on duty the night they met.

                    SILKY
               (to bartender)
          Do you remember the note you gave me that
          night?

                    BARTENDER
          Sure. Not every night a lady gets a note
          instead of a line.

                    DONOVAN
          Do you remember what the guy looked like?
          It's important.

                    BARTENDER
          Can't say that I do. What a minute. He was
          wearing a hat. It kept his face in the shadows.

                    SILKY
          Any scars, jewelry? His age?

The bartender shakes his head.

                    BARTENDER
          Sorry.

                    DONOVAN
          Let's go get something to eat.

INT. RESTAURANT/BAR - NIGHT

Silky and Donovan enter a favorite hang-out for cops. Noisy, laughter-filled, Silky
leads the way.

She sees Donovan being given the thumbs-up sign from fellow officers.

She finds them an empty booth, and slides into the seat, grabs a menu, appears to be
greatly interested in it.

Donovan slides into booth, reaches for a menu, opens it.

                    SILKY
          Don't even think of trying.

                    DONOVAN
          What's good?

                    SILKY
          I know about the contest.

Donovan scans menu.

                    DONOVAN
          What have you got against cops?

                    SILKY
          Not a thing. I am one, remember?

                    DONOVAN
          But you won't go out with one.

A WAITRESS plops two beers on the table.

                     SILKY
          The usual for me, Judy.

                    DONOVAN
          Whatever, she's having.

Waitress leaves.

                     SILKY
          I'll never marry one. I don't want to bury him.

                    DONOVAN
          What about Neil?

                     SILKY
          Nosey, aren't you?

                    DONOVAN
          Gossip. And I'm a cop.

Silky just stares at him.

                    DONOVAN (CONT'D)
          Tell me or I'll nose around.

                     SILKY
          He was a mistake. Other than that, none of
          your business. First thing tomorrow--

Donovan gets up, drags her with him by the hand to the dance floor. Only a few
couples are dancing.

From the way Silky looks around, it's obvious she's never done this before. At least,
not here.

She's getting too much attention as others start noticing. She doesn't like it. Tries to
shake loose of Donovan, but he hangs on tight, not letting go.

In the b.g., Neil and Tony enter. Right away, Tony pulls Neil back toward the door.
Neil shakes him off. They argue. Tony leaves.

                    DONOVAN
          Wonder what that was about.

                    SILKY
          They argue a lot. And always work it out.
          Friends do that, ya' know.

Donovan bends down close.

                    DONOVAN
          Dance with me Silky, or so help me I'll kiss
          you right here. In front of everyone.

                    SILKY
          You do and the force of my knee will jam
          your balls into your throat.

Donovan laughs as if he knows she'd fail. She continues to glare.

                    DONOVAN
          Tomorrow is tomorrow. Tonight is about us.

                    SILKY
          There is no us.

                    DONOVAN
          Not because you don't want it. You know you
          do.

Silky rolls her eyes.

                    SILKY
          Save me from every man who thinks he's
          every woman's answer.

                    DONOVAN
          Not every woman. Just you. You feel it too.
          Deny it.

                    SILKY
          You're full of shit. Fuck you.

Donovan twirls her on the floor.

                    DONOVAN
          Now that's the spirit. I knew you'd see it my
          way.

She stomps on his instep. He groans, bends down.

She escapes from his clutches, is back at their booth in mere seconds.

She picks up her beer and downs it.

She looks around for the waitress.

Donovan returns to the table, receives hearty slaps on the back along the way.

At the table, he makes to grab her mug, but she pulls it away from him, grabbing his empty mug too.

                              SILKY
                    My turn.

She takes the mugs to the bar, waits for the busy bartender.

Leaning against the bar, she turns sideways, sees Neil further down arguing with a seedy looking MAN, 30s, leather, sleeveless vest, tattoos everywhere.

Neil tries to hand him a piece of paper, but man won't take it. Man says something. Neil looks angry.

Man leaves.

Neil glares, wads the paper up and throws it on the floor. He leaves the bar.

Silky retrieves the paper, stuffs it in her jeans. Returns to bar. Grabs refreshed beers, heads back to the booth. Sets their drinks down.

                              SILKY (CONT'D)
                    Be right back.

Heads for the *Ladies* room.

INT. HALL TO RESTROOMS

It's dark, a pay phone at the beginning of the hall. Hall is empty.

She's almost to the *Ladies* door when she's grabbed from behind and turned around.

It's Donovan and he kisses her, catching her off guard. While she attempts to push away, she doesn't try very hard. She wants to give into the kiss but can't.

He withdraws. She starts sputtering.

                              SILKY
                    Of all the--

He drops his head toward hers again. Her gaze is on his mouth. His lips nearly at hers, he stops. She closes the distances and they're kissing again, more thoroughly than before. She's pinned against the wall, his body shielding her from view.

When they part, he has the note she had stuffed in her jeans. She grabs for it, but he holds it away from her.

                    DONOVAN
          Keeping secrets, are we?

                    SILKY
          I haven't even read it.

                    DONOVAN
          Yet, you felt it was important enough to pick
          up.

With one hand held out away from her, Donovan opens it. His whole demeanor changes. He hands it to her.

                    DONOVAN (CONT'D)
          Same fucking paper.

CLOSEUP - NOTE

"Little Miss Muffet"

                                        BACK TO SCENE

                    DONOVAN
          Trying to protect your old flame?

                    SILKY
          He's not my flame anything, and I'm not
          trying to protect him.

                    DONOVAN
          Doesn't look that way to me.

                    SILKY
          I don't give a rat's ass how it looks to you.

She glares.

Disgusted, he turns and heads back toward the booth. When he's at the end of the hall--

                    SILKY (CONT'D)
          That kiss didn't count.

Donovan spins around, eyes her up and down.

                           DONOVAN
              In your world, maybe. Counts for me.

                            SILKY
              Didn't do a damn thing for me.

Donovan walks back to her, his gaze never leaving hers, his eyes penetrating.

She's breathy heavily, her face flushed. He lowers his voice.

                           DONOVAN
              Care to let me do a moisture check?

INT. SHOOTING RANGE - LATER

Frustration is written all over Silky's body language.

Gun loaded, she takes her stance and empties it. Quickly.

She starts reloading. From the next booth, she hears fire.

She looks up and sees the bulls-eye taking direct hits, right in the heart, not one
bullet going astray from its mark.

Silence. She sticks her head around the back, around the divider. It's Randy. He sees
her and acknowledges her presence.

                            SILKY
              Quite a hand you have there.

Randy shrugs nonchalantly.

                            RANDY
              Shoot to kill, I say. Take no hostages.

INT. SILKY'S APARTMENT - FRONT DOOR - MORNING

Silky, in a nightshirt, slippers, shuffles across the room, sipping a cup of coffee.

Opens front door. Donovan stands there holding paper in his hand, other hand up
and ready to knock on the door.

She takes the paper.

                            SILKY
              That reminds me. I forgot to put the garbage
              out. Hold on and I'll get it.

She tries to shut the door as she turns, but Donovan blocks its movement, follows her in. Shuts the door behind him.

She ignores him.

                    DONOVAN
          I love a sexy woman in the morning.

                    SILKY
          What a dick.

                    DONOVAN
          Dick detective to you. Got any coffee?

                    SILKY
          Kitchen. I'll be ready in five minutes.

He takes in her disheveled hair and attire. She disappears into her bedroom and shuts the door.

                    DONOVAN
               (to himself)
          No way. No woman can be ready for anything
          in five minutes.

INT. KITCHEN

Donovan has barely poured a cup of coffee and taken a few sips when Silky's in the door, dressed, hair combed.

                                        CUT TO:

INT. MAURY DAVID'S DINING ROOM

Silky and Donovan eating breakfast with her parents. Her mother gets up and goes around refilling coffee cups.

                    DONOVAN
          Mrs. David, I can't remember when I've had a
          better breakfast.

                    MRS. DAVID
          Maybe next time, you'll try the grits.

The three Davids laugh like conspirators. Donovan frowns.

                    SILKY
          It's a Southern thing.

                    MAURY
          Don't feel bad, son. Few Yankees ever learn
          to love the stuff.

                    SILKY
          Dad, do you remember the last case Jason was
          working on?

                    MAURY
          Hard to forget. He told me he knew who had
          killed Jessica.

                    DONOVAN
          He knew and yet no one was arrested?

                    MAURY
          Told me it was a hunch. On the verge of
          verifying his clues. Then the shooting
          occurred.

                    SILKY
          But there wasn't anything in the file. Nothing
          indicating he was close to solving the case. No
          notes of any kind.

                    MAURY
          No notes?   That's funny. Jason had lots of
          notes...
                    (beat)
          Wait a minute. The boys who ended up with
          the case said it was riddled with dead ends.
          Said the file was near empty.

INT. POLICE PRECINCT - CONFERENCE ROOM

Donovan and Silky at it again, have been for a while. Trying to fill in blanks at the
blackboard. They've got the words LITTLE MISS MUFFETT as the last entry on
the board.

                    DONOVAN
          Anything back regarding Jessica's note?

                    SILKY
          On my desk.

She moves from the conference room to--

INT. POLICE REPORTING ROOM

Picks up the file from her desk. Moves past Larry's desk.

Takes a second look. A bottom drawer is slightly open. Small bits of paper. Ivory paper.

She tries to pull the drawer out further, but it sticks.

Finally, she jerks it open. She feels blindly into the back of the drawer and pulls out a plastic bag. With a bullet.

TITLED: JASON

INT. POLICE PRECINCT - CONFERENCE ROOM

She plops the file before Donovan. Then the clean sheet of paper.

                    SILKY
          Frisco's and Larry's desk. Neil uses it too.

She hands him the plastic bag, label side on the back.

                    SILKY (CONT'D)
          Found this too.

                    DONOVAN
          Looks old.

He turns the bag around. Reads the label.

                    DONOVAN (CONT'D)
          Jason?

Larry walks by.

                    SILKY
               (calling out)
          Larry.

His head appears in the door.

                    LARRY
          Yeah?

                    SILKY
          Got a minute?

He enters the room. Donovan holds up the bag with the bullet and the paper. Larry pales.

                              DONOVAN
          Tell us about the shooting.

                              SILKY
          Is that the bullet that killed Jason?

Beat.

                              LARRY
          Yeah.

                              SILKY
          Why do you have it?

                              DONOVAN
          Was a ballistics test run on it?

                              LARRY
          No.
                    (sighs)
          He was shot by that crazed robber. I was with
          Jason in the emergency room when they dug
          that out. I took it. Was going to hunt the
          bastard down. So much was going on at the
          time. I forgot about it. I was with him when
          he died.

He's in pain as if it was yesterday.

                              DONOVAN
          What about this paper?

                              LARRY
          What about it?   It was issued years ago. I've
          gotta go.

He leaves.

                              DONOVAN
          Jesus. That means anyone on the force could
          be our man.
                    (beat.)
          Including him.

                              SILKY
                    (indicating the bullet)
          How could he just forget about it?

Donovan
Ballistics will tell us more.

Neil walks past the open door. Donovan goes to the door, looks out. Sees Neil leave the building.

Donovan motions for Silky to follow. She grabs the bagged bullet, hands it off to another officer with instructions to process.

EXT. NEW ORLEANS STREET

Neighborhood is mid-lower class. Some yards nice and spruced up, others with garbage everywhere. Some houses painted, some as gray as an overcast sky.

Donovan and Silky, in one car, follow Neil. He's two cars ahead of them.

Neil pulls to the curb. Donovan does the same.

                    SILKY
          This is ridiculous.

Neil gets out of his car. Crosses street and approaches house that's dark, drab in color, run-down, in need of repair.

New chain-link fence surrounds an almost all-dirt yard.

Neil opens the gate.

Immediately, a Rottweiler is there. Neil pets it, showing no fear of the dog, whatsoever.

Donovan looks at Silky and raises an eyebrow.

                    SILKY (CONT'D)
          Doesn't mean a thing.

They continue watching.

Neil at the door. He opens it and enters, without knocking.

                    DONOVAN
          Still want to claim there's nothing of interest
          here?

Lots of foot traffic. A couple more people go into the house. A few leave.

                    DONOVAN (CONT'D)
          Drug house?

                    SILKY
          Looks like it, but Neil doesn't do drugs. Not
          his style.

                    DONOVAN
          How would you know?

                    SILKY
          I just do. And there's no way he's part of
          these murders. I'd stake my life on it.

                    DONOVAN
          No one is above suspicion. Especially when
          they write nursery rhymes on the same paper
          our killer uses.
                    (beat)
          Slide over here and kiss me.

                    SILKY
          Think again, surveillance boy--

She startles as he twists toward her, pulls her toward him, and wraps his arms around
her. She tries to get loose of his vice-like grip. One hand grabs the hair at the back of
his head and pulls him away, but only by an inch.

                    SILKY (CONT'D)
          Find someone else to knock teeth with. You
          aren't working that kind of black magic--

Donovan starts kissing her. She struggles.

EXT. CAR

POV from a passerby: It looks like the two are writhing in ecstasy.

INT. CAR

Silky talks while Donovan kisses her.

                    SILKY
          Get your hands off me, you giant octopus.

Donovan answers back, all the while his lips on hers.

                    DONOVAN
          Shut up!   We're being watched.

Lips still together.

                        SILKY
          No kidding!

She tries to look around, but his hands are holding her head in position. All she can
do is move her glance around but does so with squinty eyes. Just in case.

                        DONOVAN
          Trust me.

Lips still together.

                        SILKY
          My daddy told me to run and run fast anytime
          I heard those words uttered with testosterone.

Donovan laughs. Silky pushes away.

                        DONOVAN
          Your father's all right.

He looks out the window.

                        DONOVAN (CONT'D)
          Coast is clear.

Silky looks around seeing no one. She attempts to slug him in the jaw. His large hand
meets her fist and envelops it.

She pulls away from him as if burned.

                        SILKY
          That's twice now. A third time and you'll be
          wishing you had a bullet in you.

                        DONOVAN
          You'd be lousy at poker.

                        SILKY
          Some detective. I don't see anyone. There
          wasn't anyone.

                        DONOVAN
          There was.

He nods toward the car that is passing them.

                          DONOVAN (CONT'D)
            There.

Donovan turns ignition, pulls out. They follow.

They don't see the man, the briefest of an outline, standing in the shadows, in their
blind spot.

INT. DINER - LATER

Silky moves from *Ladies* restroom to a booth where Donovan waits. Two coffee
mugs are on the table.

Silky slides into booth. Donovan's coffee half gone already. She picks up a packet of
sugar and dumps it into her coffee, stirring.

                          SILKY
            What next, Dick Tracy?

A waitress, coffee pot in hand, goes around to all the tables, refilling. Digging into
her apron pocket, she places a few creamers on the tables.

She tops Donovan's coffee.

                          SILKY (CONT'D)
            Sure you don't want to question her.

                          DONOVAN
            For what?

                          SILKY
            She's served coffee to Neil before.

                          DONOVAN
                (to waitress)
            Thanks.

Waitress leaves.

                          DONOVAN (CONT'D)
            Anyone ever tell you that you've got a smart
            mouth.

                          SILKY
            All the time. Nothing you can do about it.

He grins, staring at her mouth.

DONOVAN
I love how you tempt me. All we need to do is
get your mouth to say what your eyes, lips,
and the rest of body are saying.

SILKY
You're disgusting.

DONOVAN
And you're in denial.

INT. POLICE PRECINCT - CONFERENCE ROOM - MORNING

Silky throws her pencil across the table. It hits the board and falls to the floor.
Donovan doesn't even look up from the file he's reading.

Many coffee cups and weary expressions. They've been there for hours.

Jack enters the room. He doesn't look happy.

JACK
There's been another murder.

Donovan slams the file folder to the table.

DONOVAN
Damn it!

SILKY
When?

JACK
Last night around eight.

SILKY
(to Donovan)
We were stalking Neil at eight.

DONOVAN
Yeah. Looks like your old boyfriend is clear.
(beat)
For now.

Just then Neil walks by. Silky calls out.

SILKY
Neil!

Neil backtracks, sticks his head back into the door.

                    DONOVAN
            Where were you last night?

Not suspecting anything, Neil is cocky, playful.

                    NEIL
        Who's asking?

Donovan, impatient, and not liking the answer, jumps up and grabs Neil's shirt, pulls
him up short.

                    DONOVAN
        Me.

Silky squirms her way between the two men, pulling Donovan's hands off Neil,
pushing Neil away, using Donovan as a brace.

No one notices that something slips out of Neil's pocket and falls to the floor.

                    SILKY
        Stop it!

Angry at being manhandled, Neil spins, takes a step away, spins around again. He's
smirking. He's going to play with Donovan.

                    NEIL
                (to Donovan)
        You got a warrant?

                    SILKY
        You know he--

                    NEIL
                (to Donovan)
        It's none of your fucking business!
                (to Silky; more gently)
        Yours either.

                    DONOVAN
            What do you know about Little Miss Muffet?

Several emotions flit across Neil's face--so quickly, they're almost missed.

                    NEIL
        She liked curds and whey.

Silky frowns. Neil leaves the room.

                    DONOVAN
          Sorry son-of-a-bitch. He's lying.

                    SILKY
          I know.

Just then, Silky sees the object on the floor, bends, and picks it up. It's a lock of coarse, dark hair tied around a nail.

                    DONOVAN
          Don't tell me. Voodoo. And you still want to
          believe he has nothing to do with it.

He picks up a file, looks at it, and throws it at the bulletin board. Papers flutter in front of the girls' pictures.

Phone rings.

Silky answers.

                    SILKY
          David here... Hi Mom... working on the case...
          no, I can't... no, tonight isn't good... no, we'll
          be working on the case... all right. We'll be
          there.

                    DONOVAN
          You caved.

                    SILKY
          And you're going with me.

                    DONOVAN
          I've never been a hostage before. Is it kinky?

INT. DAVID'S KITCHEN

Mrs. David, at the sink, takes celery and carrots from a plastic bag, arranges them on a plate.

Silky leans against the counter, facing the sink, looks out the window, snitches a carrot.

Mrs. David swats at her hand, and Silky bites off a piece, laughing.

                    MRS. DAVID
          You're as bad as your father. Whatever
          happened to that nice lieutenant?

Donovan enters the kitchen, with neither woman noticing.

                    SILKY
          The one you wanted me to date?   He got
          married.

Mrs. David looks at Silky, exasperated.

                    MRS. DAVID
          You waited too long.

Donovan reaches a hand around Mrs. David, snitching a piece of celery. She starts to swat at his hand--

                    DONOVAN
          I'm single.

--but pats it instead.

                    MRS. DAVID
          Bet you could keep my misbehaving daughter
          in line.

                    DONOVAN
          Bet I could.

                    SILKY
          Mother!

                    MRS. DAVID
          Here.

She hands Donovan the tray of vegetables. He winks at her.

Silky picks up the dip. Mrs. David pushes them out of her kitchen. Together.

                    MRS. DAVID (CONT'D)
          Tell Father fifteen minutes. Becky and Jenny
          will be here any minute.

INT. DAVID'S DINING ROOM

As Donovan and Silky pass through.

                    DONOVAN
          You only want me for my body.
               (beat)
          For protection against your mother.

Silky looks surprised. Like she's been found out.

                    DONOVAN (CONT'D)
          My mother goes down that same road. You've
          seen one mother, you've seen them all.

                    SILKY
          You've got a mother?

INT. DAVID'S DINING ROOM- LATER

Donovan, Silky, Maury, Becky, Jenny, Jenny's husband, and Mrs. David are getting
up from the table, dinner over. Maury grabs a cane and walks with a distinct limp.

                    MAURY
          That was great, Mother.

Everyone else echoes their thanks and sentiments. All the David's, except Maury,
start clearing the table. Mrs. David takes Donovan's dishes from him.

                    MRS. DAVID
          You're a guest. Go find something on TV.

                    MAURY
          I'll get the beer.

INT. DAVID'S LIVING ROOM

Donovan strolls in, circles around the room, looks at pictures on the walls and
tables.

Maury enters, notices Donovan's attraction to the pictures. He hands Donovan a
beer.

                    MAURY
          She was quite the tomboy. Only girl in an
          extended family of all boys.

Maury puffs up a little, smiling.

                    MAURY (CONT'D)
          She was a tough little scrapper. Had a right
          hook that was a killer.

Still does judging how close we've come to meeting.

                    MAURY (CONT'D)
          (laughs)
     After a few broken noses, the boys learned to
     keep their distance when taunting.
          (beat)
     It was hard for Mother when Silk decided to
     be a cop. Mother has her heart set on seeing
     our little girl in a wedding dress. Broke
     Mother's heart when she broke off the
     engagement.

                    DONOVAN
     She ever say why?

                    MAURY
     No. Carl and I were disappointed too. Like
     Neil and Silky, he and I grew up together.
          (Maury smiles, remembering)

                    MAURY (CONT'D)
     Learned how to shoot back behind his
     grandpa's old tobacco barn.
          (beat)
     That's when we decided to be cops. Only
     fourteen at the time.
          (chuckles)
     His grandmother caught us one time. She
     handled a switch better than Carl handled
     guns. Whooeeee. You never wanted to get too
     close to that woman.

Donovan laughs. Maury sighs.

                    MAURY (CONT'D)
     I miss those days. There wasn't a case we
     couldn't solve. How's your case going?

                    DONOVAN
     We need a break.

                    MAURY
     Stop trying so hard. Ready for another beer?

Donovan nods, starts to get up.

                    MAURY (CONT'D)
     Sit down, son. I'll get 'em. It'll let Mother see
     I'm getting some exercise.

Maury leaves the room.

Donovan sits back on the couch, arms outstretched on the back of the couch. He looks around the room, looks at the pictures again.

Suddenly, his demeanor changes. He sits forward, alert, eyes darting from photo to photo of a much younger Silky.

He gets up and reaches for one of the photos that rests on the piano.

CLOSEUP of Silky, at 15, smiling into the camera.

INT. POLICE PRECINCT - CONFERENCE ROOM

Donovan tacks the picture of Silky on the chalkboard.

                    SILKY
          Where'd you get--

                    DONOVAN
          Took it from your dad's house...

He puts a finger to her lips to shush her as she gets ready to blast him verbally.

                    DONOVAN (CONT'D)
          --with your mother's approval.

Silky rolls her eyes.

                    DONOVAN (CONT'D)
          Notice anything?

Silky looks at all the pictures, including the one of herself.

                    SILKY
          All I see are young girls.
          Attractive young girls.

                    DONOVAN
          You don't see it?

                    SILKY
          No.

                    DONOVAN
          Anyone of those girls could have been you.

Silky's frowns but isn't buying it.

                    DONOVAN (CONT'D)
Right down to the eye color, hair color and
features. Slight variations, I'll admit, but even
their hair is like yours.

                    SILKY
Why would anyone want to kill me?
          (beat)
You're full of shit. There were girls murdered
when I was a kid.

                    DONOVAN
The same age as you. Each and every time. I
can't explain it either, but the similarities are
too great to ignore.

                    SILKY
No more than you can ignore Neil being
involved, right?   You're a piece of work,
Donovan. What did you do, kiss the Blarney
Stone before you came over on the ship?

                    DONOVAN
You've got enemies around here-- right in this
precinct, and you don't even know it.

                    SILKY
Oh, I know it all right. I've been facing those
so-called enemies every day since I got my
badge. Even before that. But you're talking
about a vicious killer, not some boy/manchild
who's jealous because I have breasts instead
of a dick.
          (beat)
I'll admit in the beginning, I had a point to
prove. I was as good as them, and I earned
any promotion I got. I want to be detective
because I'm good.

Donovan starts thumbing through the nursery rhyme book, reciting from "Hush
Little Baby."

                    DONOVAN
Hush, little baby, don't say a word,--

Silky starts to sing the words softly.

                    SILKY
          Papa's going to buy you a mocking bird. If
          that mocking bird won't sing, Papa's going to
          buy you a...

Her voice gets even softer, barely audible.

                    SILKY (CONT'D)
          ...diamond ring.

SILKY'S DREAM

Silky is wide awake, eyes open, gazing straight ahead, seeing nothing but the images
in her mind. She's 7, holds out her hand. A multi-carat diamond (paste) ring is
dropped into her hand.

MALE VOICE O.S.

It's a diamond for you. He grabs her. We only see black clothing, see him from
chest-level down.

INT. POLICE PRECINCT - CONFERENCE ROOM - PRESENT

Silky screams.

                    SILKY
          Stop it!

Donovan is shaking her.

                    DONOVAN
          Silky!
               (softly)
          Silky.

Her eyes filled with horror. She tries fighting him.

Then she recognizes him and collapses against him.

He holds her while she takes huge gulps of breath, a sob or two coming out in-
between.

Finally, she's regained her composure. She pulls away, looking down. Finally, she
looks up, her face anguished.

                    SILKY
          He's taunting me.

                    DONOVAN
          Who?

                     SILKY
          I never see his face.

Randy enters the room, a grim look on his face.

Before he can say anything to them, a ruckus from the reporting office area. All three
come out of the conference room.

INT. POLICE REPORTING ROOM

Jenny talking in screams. Two policemen on either side. Several people trying to calm
her, to get her to sit.

She claws at everyone, unable to be controlled. She sees Silky. They meet.

                     JENNY
          They've got her!   They've got my baby.

Jenny collapses to the floor. Silky goes down with her, supporting her. Donovan is
instantly behind Jenny, also supporting her.

                  JENNY (CONT'D)
          Becky is missing.

Donovan lifts Jenny up in his arms, shushing her, trying to calm her.

Heads to Guidry's office.

Guidry enters the room, observes everyone at a glance. Sees Donovan carrying
Jenny. He follows Silky into--

INT. GUIDRY'S OFFICE.

--where Donovan sets Jenny on the couch. She's sobbing.

                   DONOVAN
               (to Guidry)
          She needs some water.

Guidry goes. Silky sits next to Jenny, puts her arm around her, holds her hand.

Donovan sits on the coffee table, faces Jenny. Guidry returns with the water.
Donovan makes her drink. Jenny hands him the glass.

                    SILKY
          Honey, what happened? Start at the
          beginning.

Jenny takes a deep breath.

                    JENNY
          We went to the zoo--

She talks to Silky, ignoring the men.

                    JENNY (CONT'D)
          --you know how she loves that place.

                    SILKY
          Yes. I know.

                    JENNY
          One minute she was right there with me. The
          next minute--
                    (she sobs)
          --she was gone.

                    GUIDRY
                    (to Donovan and Silky)
          Officers just told me she insisted she be
          brought here.
                    (to Jenny)
          What was she wearing?

                    JENNY
          White shorts, a red top, tennis shoes. Her
          favorite bracelet. I thought she went to the
          bathroom. I waited, even got people to help
          me look. But she's gone.

                    DONOVAN
          You said they. What did you mean?

                    JENNY
          I found this where she was last standing.

Jenny digs in a pocket and comes out with a scrap of paper. She holds it out to Silky.

Silky takes from it from Jenny, carefully, so as not to put her prints on the paper.

Guidry races to his desk, opens a drawer, grabs a bag, shakes it out, hands it to Silky.

She bags it, reads it.

                    DONOVAN
          You didn't give this to the officers?

Jenny shakes her head.

                    JENNY
          So much confusion.

She hands it to Guidry, who reads it, hands it to Donovan.

CLOSE-UP on note:

"To market, to market"

                                        BACK TO SCENE

EXT. FARMER'S MARKET - DAY

Located on the fringes of the French Quarter, the market is filled with tourists and locals shopping.

Donovan, Silky, Larry, Randy, Frisco, Jack, and several other cops go in and around stalls, searching, drawing the attention of anyone and everyone in the market.

Donovan stops by a table, stoops, pulls a handkerchief out of his pocket, and picks something up with it. Something hidden by boxes stacked at the table.

By the time Silky is at his side, he's standing, holding a cloth hand-made doll with non-descript features.

A piece of jewelry is around its neck. A giant pin stuck through its face between the eyes.

                    DONOVAN
          A tourist dropped it.

                    SILKY
          I don't think so.

She points the silver necklace around the dolls neck.

                    SILKY (CONT'D)
          It's Becky's bracelet. I gave it to her.

INT. VOODOO MUSEUM

A few customers stroll in. Donovan and Silky are at the counter with Banjo. The doll in a bag.

                    BANJO
          Been a long time since these eyes seen one
          like this. 'Bout 20 years ago. When old Maudie
          died.

Banjo hands the doll back to Silky.

                    BANJO (CONT'D)
          She was a seamstress. A box of these dolls
          was found in the house. No one ever claimed
          them.

                    SILKY
          I remember Granny talking about her. Said
          she was the best seamstress in the county.
          Was she involved in black magic?

                    BANJO
          I doubt it. But there was someone who was.
          Just starting out then.

                    DONOVAN
          Who?

                    BANJO
          Never heard a name. Check with the papa-loa.

                    DONOVAN
          The what?

                    SILKY
                (to Donovan)
          Voodoo priest
                (to Banjo)
          Thanks.
                (to Donovan)
          Come on, time's running out.

She leaves the store quickly, abruptly, with Donovan behind. Donovan's at the door
when Banjo's words stop him--

                    BANJO
          You can't protect her, Goliath.

                    DONOVAN
          Like hell, I can't.

EXT. BAYOU - DAY

Donovan and Silky in small boat, motor up. They're paddling.

Donovan sits in the front, nervously looking around. Silky is very much at home.

Moss hangs from the trees. Lots of animal noises: croaks, bird cries, movement in nearby bushes, the grunt of a gator.

Suddenly, Donovan shrieks, combatting the air with his paddle. He starts shifting from side to side, ducking.

> SILKY
> Pink elephants?

> DONOVAN
> Spider's. Unnecessary creatures.

> SILKY
> Gators don't bother you then?

Donovan looks around frantically.

> DONOVAN
> Where?

Only then does Donovan see several gators lying on shore, mouths gaped open. One slides into the water.

> DONOVAN (CONT'D)
> They can't bite through the boat, can they?

> SILKY
> Ever see Jaws?

Donovan holds the paddle like a weapon now.

> SILKY (CONT'D)
> Stop rocking the boat. Put that paddle to use,
> in the water.

Tentatively, Donovan starts to paddle again, his gaze on the gators.

EXT. BAYOU DOCK

Boat smacks up against a dock. Out of the boat, they cross a shaky footbridge.

> DONOVAN
> Not exactly the Hilton.

EXT. BAYOU LAND - WILD

Once on ground, they pass posts with strange markings and odd objects handing from the posts.

                    DONOVAN
          What's this, the welcome sign?

                    SILKY
          You're entering the houmfort or Hounfour, a
          religious compound.

EXT. HOUMFORT

A large, round, open-air wooden structure on the right dominates the compound, posts supporting a tin roof, earth packed floor.

A wall about knee-high circles its perimeter, with an opening.

Centered inside the structure is a pole painted with bright rainbow colors in spiral bands.

At the base of the pole is a flat-topped base of cement used as an altar, covered with candles, food, stones, beads, drums.

On the left, a wooded square house.

In the center of the compound, a fire burns and in the middle of the fire is an iron rod.

Suddenly, JOBY JOHNSON, a man with only one eye, aged somewhere between forever and infinity, dressed in all white, appears out of nowhere.

Silky walks to Joby, gives him a hug.

Donovan relaxes.

                    JOBY
          Thought you'd moved out of the country or
          something.

                    SILKY
          Just working. Joby, this is Donovan, my new
          partner.
                    (to Donovan)
          This is Joby, the papa-loa.

Donovan and Joby shake hands.

                    JOBY
          I knew you were coming.

                    DONOVAN
          You can predict the future?

                    JOBY
          No. You made enough noise in the bayou to
          resurrect the dead.

Raindrops fall. Joby leads the way to the round structure.

Under the roof, the rain becomes a downpour.

                    JOBY (CONT'D)
          You approach every church alter this way?
          With disbelief?

Donovan raises an eyebrow, questioning.

                    JOBY (CONT'D)
          People don't understand voodoo, and what
          they don't understand they're afraid of.

He unfolds a camp chair, indicating Silky to sit. He gives one to Donovan and sits on
a third.

                    DONOVAN
          What do you know of black magic?

                    SILKY
          Specifically, around here?

                    JOBY
          There's a very powerful houngan in the city.
          In the resurrected secret sect, Bizango.

                    DONOVAN
          Houngan?

                    SILKY
          A priest, like Joby. Only this one is Bokor--
          evil.

                    JOBY
          He's getting strong. Evil beyond anything I've
          seen before. This man is at the center of the
          murders. Becky is still alive.

Donovan glances at Silky.

                    SILKY
          No one's told him anything.

                    DONOVAN
          How do you know that?

                    JOBY
          I've 'seen' her. She's afraid, but alive.

                    SILKY
          He doesn't travel. He has visions.

As suddenly as it started, the rain stops.

Water drips from the roof. Steam rises from the ground, off the roof.

                    JOBY
               (to Silky)
          The answers are within. Heart. Soul. Head.

She pauses. Frowns.

When he rises, Donovan and Silky do too. Joby hands Donovan a small black bag,
with a long string on it.

                    JOBY (CONT'D)
          Silky already knows our way, knows how to
          protect herself. This will protect you.

Donovan looks at it strangely.

                    SILKY
          You wear it around your neck.

Donovan starts to open the bag. Silky puts out her hand to stop him.

                    SILKY (CONT'D)
          Later.

                    JOBY
          It'll fix what's not right you, Shooter.

Donovan is clearly unnerved by Joby words and by not knowing the contents of the
bag.

He holds it out, away from his body, like it has cooties or could bite.

EXT. CITY STREET - NIGHT

Donovan and Silky's car enters the city again.

INT. CAR

Donovan's bag hangs from the rearview mirror. He eyes it nervously as he makes a turn.

                    SILKY
          Don't even think of moving it.

                    DONOVAN
          What's in it?

                    SILKY
          Promise not to move it?

                    DONOVAN
          All right, I promise.

EXT. CAR TRAVELING

                    SILKY
          Spiders to start with.

The car swerves.

                    SILKY (CONT'D)
          Dead ones!

EXT. STREET

Where they had staked out Neil, the house with the new chain- link fence.

Marked cars surround the area.

They stop. Randy and Jack meet them. Cops are moving handcuffed prisoners to cars. Other cops are moving toward the house.

To an outsider, the scene looks like mass confusion.

                    RANDY
          It's a drug bust. I've discovered something
          about your case you should know about.

Donovan, sees Neil come out of the house, his hands cuffed.

                              DONOVAN
                    What's he doing here?

Randy turns, to see what Donovan sees.

In the b.g. shadows, a car with no lights pulls up, a MAN gets out, surveys the scene
and reaches in the car for--

                               RANDY
                    The back is rented to a--

--a gun, semi-automatic goes off. Bullets everywhere.

All hell breaks loose.

Everyone hits the ground.

Donovan covers Silky with his body. More shots.

Cops everywhere shoot at the shooter. The man drops.

Eerie silence.

Cops surround the shooter.

Neil is dragged back up to his feet by a cop.

Silky raises her head. Randy nearby, on his back, his eyes stare skyward.

                               SILKY
                    Nooooo!

She scrambles out from under Donovan. He tries to restrain her, then sees Randy,
too. He moves quickly with Silky, but his eyes dart, looking everywhere.

Silky concentrates on her former partner. Then she sees Jack, next to him. He's lying
face down, not moving.

                           SILKY (CONT'D)
                    Shit. Check on Jack.

Donovan moves to Jack.

Turns him over.

A bullet hole in forehead. Eyes open. Dead.

Donovan closes Jack's eyes. He moves back to Randy.

Randy's alive, but barely. Silky cradles his head in her lap. He's shot in the chest. She puts pressure on his wound with her hand.

DONOVAN
We need some an ambulance here!

Randy clutches Donovan's arm. SIRENS in the background.

RANDY
(to Donovan)
Neil knows who...

Randy passes out. Silky moans.

SILKY
Don't you die!   Don't you dare die!

EMT's are there, take over.

Silky moves back. They go to work on him. He's quickly put on a stretcher.

EXT. STREET - LATER

Silky stands watching. In the f.g. ambulance door is shut.

Officer hits the door. Ambulance takes off, with SIREN.

Neil is visible, in their line of sight.

Silky, seeing him, marches toward him. Her gaze never wavers. Her jaw tightens. She's angry.

Neil looks around the scene in misery, shaken to the core. He sees Silky approach. He stands his ground, but nervously.

She's in his face, visibly shaken, lets her anger take over.

SILKY
Miss Muffet. Explain it. Now!

NEIL
It's a fucking horse. A goddamn fucking horse
that cost me thousands.

DONOVAN
And the little charm you dropped?

He pulls the nail and hair out of his pocket.

                    NEIL
          A good luck charm. You're seeing phantom
          nursery rhymes.

Silky pulls her right hand back and with a fist, socks him in the jaw. She shakes her
hand immediately, in pain. Another officer keeps Neil from going down to the
ground.

                    OFFICER
          Nice hook.

Suddenly Guidry is there. Sees Neil, the cuffs.

                    GUIDRY
          What the hell?

                    NEIL
          Leave it alone, Dad. Just leave it alone. Don't
          fix it. Don't even try.

                    SILKY
             (to Neil)
          Who's the shooter?

Neil looks over at him.

                    NEIL
          A disgruntled bookie. I was trying to warn
          them inside.

Neil's led to a squad car and put into backseat.

Guidry starts toward the car. Neil shakes his head. The car drives off.

Guidry turns and faces Silky. Controlled anger.

                    GUIDRY
          I want to know what's going on.

                    SILKY
          So do I.

INT. GUIDRY'S OFFICE- LATER

Donovan, Silky, Frisco, and Larry stand around the room. No one looks happy.

                         GUIDRY
          Mardi Gras starts in a week and you've got
          nothing. Media's making this a three-ring
          circus and you're all the clowns.

INT. POLICE PRECINCT - CONFERENCE ROOM - LATE NIGHT

Silky is asleep in a chair, her feet on the table, files in her lap. Donovan goes through
other files.

SILKY'S DREAM

She's a child again. Her hand outstretched again. Huge diamond dropped in her hand
again. She looks down at it.

PAN to her face. Only it's not her face. It's Becky's.

                                                      DREAM ENDS

Silky awakens suddenly, stand ups, files spilling to the floor.

Donovan jumps to his feet, immediately concerned, going to Silky. Her eyes are
huge, she's perspiring.

                         SILKY
          Don't let him hurt her like he did me!

Donovan sits her back down, talking softly.

                         DONOVAN
          What did you see?

                         SILKY
          I don't know. I saw me. Only it wasn't me. It
          was Becky. He's going to hurt her. Oh, god,
          why can't I remember?

She moans, her hands cover her face. She rocks back and forth.

                         DONOVAN
          What aren't you telling me?

                         SILKY
          It's a memory that I've forgotten. I think. I
          don't know. I keep seeing pieces. Of
          something.

Donovan frowns.

                    DONOVAN
          You need to--

                    SILKY
          I don't need to do anything!

She stands and starts pacing.

                    SILKY (CONT'D)
          Shit. This isn't good, is it?

Donovan shakes his head.

                    SILKY (CONT'D)
          You can't tell anyone.

                    DONOVAN
          Only if you agree--

                    SILKY
          To see someone.

                    DONOVAN (CONT'D)
          To see someone.

INT. HOSPITAL - DAY

Donovan and Silky enter a private room. Randy's connected to a breathing machine, lots of tubes, eyes closed.

Silky, at his bedside, holds his hand, rubs her thumb on the back of his hand.

                    SILKY
          Randy?   You've got to wake up.
               (to Donovan)
          He knows. I know he knows.

Donovan leans against the wall, his arms and feet crossed. He's willing to stand there for a long time.

EXT. NEW ORLEANS - STREET - DAY

People line the streets. A funeral procession holds their interests.

Hundreds of cops, in dress uniform, walk in unison. Silky and Donovan are in front as is Guidry.

Behind are Larry and Frisco. Silky's face is grim, her pain obvious.

EXT. GRAVEYARD

Larry, Frisco, and Guidry are nowhere to be seen. On the outskirts of the group are Maury and Mrs. David.

                    MINISTER
          We commit, Jack, to his final--

A woman, dressed in black and with a veil, sobs, her legs give out under her. She's caught by several people and helped away.

Silky observes it all, her face hard, no tears in sight.

Donovan watches Silky watch the woman.

Service ends.

Tony, in plain clothes, moves through the crowd. He carries an envelope. He searches, looking for someone. He sees Silky, goes to her side.

Silky's surprised to see him. He hands her the envelope. She opens it and reads. Donovan reads over her shoulder.

                    SILKY
          Jeezus.
                    (looking around)
          Where's Dad?

Donovan, from his taller perspective, sees him.

                    DONOVAN
          Over by the tree.

SECONDS LATER -

Silky hands the paper to her father. Puzzled, he takes it and reads.

                    MAURY
          The bullet that killed Jack--

                    SILKY
          --came from the same gun that killed Jason.

                    DONOVAN
          And injured you and Randy.

                    MAURY
          That's impossible. That means--

                              SILKY
              The shooter the other day didn't fire those
              bullets. Not his gun.

                              DONOVAN
              Cops and girls from the same gun?

                              MAURY
              There were only four of us and the robber
              that night.

Silky looks around. Frowns.

                              SILKY
              He's gone.

EXT. GARDEN DISTRICT - HOUSE

Silky knocks on the door. She's impatient, peers into the windows.

Looks like no one's home.

                              DONOVAN
              Ever been inside before?

                              SILKY
              Many times. And yet...
                    (beat)
              Where is he?

Donovan tries the knob. It's turns. Donovan hesitates, looks to Silky. Silky nods. He opens the door wider, looking in cautiously.

INT. HALLWAY

Donovan and Silky slip inside the house and shut the door noiselessly behind them.

INT. LIVING ROOM

They peer into the room. Silky immediately sees a stained- glass picture on the wall. She freezes.

SILKY'S DREAM

It's the same house, same living room.

MALE VOICE O.S.
Jack and Jill went up the hill--

BACK TO SCENE

Donovan starts to speak. Immediately, Silky shushes him. She crouches. Donovan
mimics her. Now they're whispering.

SILKY
This is the house in my dreams.

They both pull out their guns.

They move through the house, hugging walls, peering around corners.

They reach a closed door. Donovan moves to the other side of it. He nods.

She opens it... quietly.... slowly. It's pitch black. Silky crouches and moves in. She
shines a flashlight around. No one's there.

Donovan flips a light switch on. The walls are black, the window blacked out.
There's nothing but a table, set up like an altar.

Above the table is more stained glass. This is the "church altar" in Silky's dreams.

They approach it. Silky lowers her gun, her eyes fastened on the altar itself. There's
something black and furry.

DONOVAN
Dead cat.

He turns it over.

DONOVAN (CONT'D)
Heart's gone.

The soft SOUND OF DRUMS suddenly starts throbbing throughout the house.
Silky covers her ears. She doesn't want to hear it.

Donovan nudges her, indicating for her to follow.

She's a cop again and follows. They move from the room, and go into--

INT. KITCHEN

No one's there. They approach another closed door. Each on either side of the door,
Silky opens it quickly.

Broom closet.

An ironing board starts to slip out. Donovan grabs it, and pushes it back in, shutting the door.

There's one more closed door.

As they approach it, DRUMS get louder.

Donovan slowly twists the doorknob, pushes the door open.

INT. SERVANTS' STAIRWAY UP

Pitch black.

Donovan is about to turn on his flashlight. Silky grabs his arm, shaking her head.

She takes the lead.

She hugs one wall going up the stairs.

She indicates for him to hug the other wall.

Too late he plants a foot in the middle of one stair. It SQUEAKS.

They freeze.

DRUMS continue.

MALE LAUGHTER and SOFT SOBBING.

INT. UPSTAIRS HALL

At the top of the stairs, a sliver of light comes from one of the doors.

They approach, one on either side. The door is ajar slightly.

Silky moves to the opening.

CLOSE ANGEL - SILKY'S POV

One bare light bulb illuminates the room. Black walls, floor and ceiling with voodoo markings on the floor.

Iron bed, bare except for a mattress covered with plastic.

Becky sits on the bed, gagged, her hands and feet tied. She appears alone in the room.

Silky opens the door. Becky's eyes widen with relief but with fear also. Becky tries to speak, but can't, and shakes her head.

Silky, relieved to find Becky, moves into--

INT. BEDROOM

--the room. Instantly, hands from the other side of the door grab her. Quickly, she's made a human shield.

Guidry holds her tightly in front of him, a gun to Silky's head.

He cocks it.

He moves them both toward Becky. Donovan fills the door way, his gun on Guidry.

                    GUIDRY
          Drop it.

Donovan doesn't. Guidry laughs.

                    GUIDRY (CONT'D)
          You're not a threat. You won't shoot.

Silky struggles. Guidry tightens his arm around her neck, choking her.

                    GUIDRY (CONT'D)
               (to Silky)
          You always thought you were better than
          Neil, even when you were kids. Always had to
          be tougher. Always had to be the best. You
          dumped him. Didn't give him a chance in bed
          or in the patrol car.

                    SILKY
          Neil is gay. He wanted our marriage as a cover
          for his lifestyle.

Guidry's look is incredulous.

                    GUIDRY
          You're lying!

                    SILKY
          Ask him yourself.

                    DONOVAN
          You killed your best friend's son.

                    GUIDRY
          Too smart for their own good. All of them.
          Jason was too close to discovering who I was.

                    SILKY
          So you set him up.

                    GUIDRY
          One bullet. Through the heart.

                    SILKY
          Same as you'll get.

Guidry laughs. He shoves Silky into Donovan's line of fire, and grabs Becky so she's
his shield now.

He moves his arms so the hand holding the gun, is the arm going around Becky.

With his other hand, he pulls a switchblade out of his pocket. He snaps it open and
holds it in such a fashion that he could stab Becky. Becky cries out.

                    SILKY (CONT'D)
          No!

Guidry moves the knife to Becky's throat.

                    GUIDRY
          I'll never give her up. I'm protected. The gods
          are on my side now. She's my sacrifice
          tonight.

Silky growls and throws herself at Guidry. He twists to thwart her off, exposes
himself for a brief second.

Donovan fires.

Guidry, Silky, and Becky are all thrust backward.

Silky hits her head on the bed rail. Guidry's back is smacked against the bed post.
SNAP.

Guidry and Silky land on the floor. Becky, sobbing, rolls into a ball and moves away
from Guidry.

Guidry face up, eyes closed, mouth a grimace of a smile.

Silky on the floor, face-down, motionless.

Donovan rushes over, gun points at Guidry, ready to fire if necessary.

Guidry's eyes open. His smile turns sinister.

> GUIDRY (CONT'D)
> You missed.

He sighs, blood comes from his mouth, and oozes through his chest, through black shirt. He's dead.

Donovan ungags Becky, unties her hands. All the while, Becky looks toward Silky, fearing the worst.

> DONOVAN
> You okay?

Becky sniffles, nods. Donovan turns to Silky. He runs his hands over her. Feeling nothing broken, he turns her over, runs his hands over her again. Her eyes open.

> SILKY
> (groans)
> Typical male. Do anything for a grope.

She groans. Tries to sit up. Groans again, holding her head. Donovan fingers her head, looks, searches.

Finds tender spot. She grimaces, slaps his hands away.

> SILKY (CONT'D)
> Don't do that. It hurts.

Becky's right there, hugs Silky.   Silky hugs back, then pushes her away to look at her.

> SILKY (CONT'D)
> Did he touch you?   Did he hurt you?

> BECKY
> No. He threatened to.

Silky draws Becky to her again. Hugs her tight.

Donovan pulls both of them up, moving them out of the room, away from the crime scene.

> CUT TO:

EXT. FRENCH QUARTER

Mardi Gras in full swing.

EXT. BAR - NIGHT

INT. BAR - HALLWAY

Randy and Silky lean against the wall. Randy smokes a cigarette. Silky is dressed like a
hooker again.

                         SILKY
            I'm surprised your doctor lets you smoke.

                         RANDY
            The lung only collapsed. I didn't break it.
            Heard Donovan's leaving.

                         SILKY
            Yeah, wanted to avoid the crowds.

Silky looks out at the crowd. She squints like she's concentrating on keying in on
individuals.

                         SILKY (CONT'D)
            Looks like it's going to a long night. Glad this
            is my last night on vice.

                         RANDY
            Congratulations on the promotion. Still seeing
            the shrink?

                         SILKY
            One more visit. Then I'll be--

Silky raises her hands, uses first two fingers on each hand to make quote marks.

                         SILKY (CONT'D)
            --cured.

                         RANDY
            Is anybody in this business ever cured?

                         SILKY
            Doc says I locked it all out. Was in
            psychological denial
                    (beat)
            Can't believe I ever admired him.

                         RANDY
              He was afraid of you. Even then.

Silky shakes her head.

                         SILKY
              I blocked everything and because of me, he
              took it out on others.
                         (beat)
              Come on, let's do this.

She moves to the bar, to her usual seat. Middle stool, with the mirror in front of her
so she can see who's approaching from behind.

No one else sits at the bar yet. A bartender plants a drink in front of her. She starts
to pick it up, then sets it back down. Her heart isn't in it.

INT. BAR - LATER

Bar is crowded. Lots of folks on dance floor, at the bar.

Silky has hooked a live one. She's almost got him reeled in when she looks in the
mirror and freezes.

Donovan stands in the doorway. To her potential customer--

                         SILKY
              Fuck off.

                         CUSTOMER
              But that's what I want to do, Sugar.

                         SILKY
              I'm a cop.

Customer catapults off the bar stool. Fast. He nearly trips.

                         CUSTOMER
              Jesus!   I didn't do anything. Really.

Silky watches Donovan. He stands, not moving.

Finally, slowly, sexily, she spins her stool around, and smiles coyly.

She pats the empty bar seat next to her.

Slowly, Donovan crosses the room.

The entire time, their gazes lock on each other.

Donovan sits. He spins her chair around so her knees are inside of his spread legs.

                    SILKY
          Sorry you didn't get the job. When do you
          leave?

                    DONOVAN
          Got as far as the airport.

Beat

                    SILKY
          But--

                    DONOVAN
          Detective David.
                    (beat)
          Sometimes you don't know what you want
          until you're about to lose it.

In the blink of an eye he has her cuffed to him.

                    SILKY
          What the hell?

He opens up his hand.

CLOSEUP - HIS PALM WITH THE KEY

                                        BACK TO SCENE

                    DONOVAN
          Your choice.

She eyes the key, eyes him.

Picks up the key, moves her hand toward the cuff. Then throws the key over her shoulder.

She shrugs.

With a sweep of his arm, Donovan clears the bar of anything and everything. All CRASHES to the floor.

Top cleared, Donovan lifts and lays Silky on the bar, then lays on top of her, his weight on his arms as he looks down at her.

The bar quiets, all eyes are on them.

                    DONOVAN (CONT'D)
There's no turning back. This is forever.

                    SILKY
Your job--

                    DONOVAN
I got made detective, too. Partner.

                    SILKY
I'm never going to live this down at the
precinct.

                    DONOVAN
I'm counting on it.

They kiss. She breaks it off. Digs for something between them. She fumbles at his
shirt, feeling something underneath.

                    SILKY
          What the hell?

She rips his shirt apart, not caring that buttons spray, hitting various customers,
plopping into drinks.

Shirt open, she pulls out a necklace, an amulet, a vile filled with amber liquid. She
looks up at him in amazement.

                    SILKY (CONT'D)
          A love potion?   You?

                    DONOVAN
          It worked.

They smile, kiss deeply and thoroughly, oblivious to everyone else.

Business as normal.

Bartender hands waitress two beers, passing them over Silky's and Donovan's prone
bodies.

Two customers sit at the end of the bar.

                    FIRST CUSTOMER
          I thought you said nothing ever happens here.

                         SECOND CUSTOMER
                    (lifts up his beer)
                It don't.

                                        FADE OUT

ABOUT THE AUTHOR

Diana Stout, MFA, Ph.D. is an award-winning screenwriter, author, and former English professor, whose writing led her into academic teaching. Her students would say, "She smiles when she talks about writing." Published in multiple genres, Stout has written romance novels, published magazine articles and short stories, is a former magazine and newspaper columnist, optioned a Hollywood screenplay, and had several short plays produced in New York city. She is a contest judge for screenwriting organizations and enjoys helping other writers learn the craft. When not writing, she enjoys reading, watching movies, jigsaw puzzles, and visiting family and friends.

OTHER TITLES

Grendel's Mother

Shattered Dreams: A Laurel Ridge Novella (#1)

Determined Hearts

Love's New Beginnings

Tomorrow's Wish for Love

Maggie's Story

The Super Simple Easy Basic Cookbook

Lost and Found - anthology

FOLLOW DIANA STOUT

Sharpened Pencils Productions LLC: sharpenedpencilsproductions.com
Facebook: facebook.com/writerDianaStout
Twitter: twitter.com/ScreenWryter13
Pinterest: pinterest.com/drdianastout
Goodreads goodreads.com/user/show/43124185-diana-stout
Instagram: instagram.com/authordianastout
BookBub: bookbub.com/authors/diana-stout

Blogs

Behind the Scenes – life as a writer: dianastout.net
Into the Core – paranormal experiences: dianastout.com
Behind the Scenes with Diana Stout and Featured Guests: dianastout.org

Reviews Made Easy

Did you like this particular book?

Please help other readers discover this book.

Did you know that you can use the same review on other websites where this book is sold or downloaded?

A review doesn't have to be long.

Feel free to use any of the below prompts to help with a review. Use as many or as few as needed.

I recommend this book because...

The first thing that drew me in to this story was:

My favorite character was [insert character name]. I liked this character because:

My favorite part of the story was when:

I like Diana's writings because:

Don't like writing a review? Rankings without a review work, too.

Thank you for reading this story. I hope you enjoyed it.